VIOLA CANALES

ORANGE CANDY SLICES

AND OTHER SECRET TALES

VIOLA CANALES

ORANGE CANDY SLICES

AND OTHER SECRET TALES

PIÑATA BOOKS
ARTE PÚBLICO PRESS
HOUSTON, TEXAS

This volume is made possible through grants from the City of Houston through the Houston Arts Alliance, the Andrew W. Mellon Foundation, and the National Endowment for the Arts (a federal agency).

Piñata Books are full of surprises!

Piñata Books
An imprint of
Arte Público Press
University of Houston
452 Cullen Performance Hall
Houston, Texas 77204-2004

Cover illustration and design by Giovanni Mora.

Canales, Viola.
    Orange candy slices and other secret tales / Viola Canales.
        p.   cm.
    ISBN 978-155885-332-4
    1. Mexican American families—Fiction.   2. Grandmothers—
Fiction.   3. Girls—Fiction.   I. Title.
    PS3603.A53 O73   2001
    813'.6—dc21   2001032872
                                                              CIP

Printed in the United States of America
September 2010–October 2010
Versa Press, Inc., East Peoria, IL
12 11 10 9 8 7 6 5 4

Contents

*To the memory of my beloved
and magical grandmothers,
Cecilia Canales
and
Lile Casas*

Orange Candy Slices

I force myself to ring the doorbell. When my aunt finally comes to the door, I look at her, then quickly look down at the ground. I hate myself for being so shy. My aunt waits patiently as I shift my weight from one leg to the other and look every which way, except at her. She asks me if I have come to play with Freddie, her son. I say no. Pasting words and sounds and awkward gestures together, I manage to ask her if she will let me cut the two flowers growing in front of her house. She lets me cut them. I take my round-edged scissors from my pocket, and carefully cut the stems in a diagonal.

It was my grandmother who taught me how to cut flowers. You first take the flower gently in your hand. Then you enjoy it by smelling it, touching it, and studying its shape and color. Once the flower feels that you are its friend, you whisper to it that you have chosen it, because of its delicate beauty, to honor the Virgin. The flower then wants you to cut it because there is no greater honor for a flower than to give itself over to the glorification of the Virgin. Then, as painlessly as you can, you cut the little stem in a slant so the flower can drink its water better.

When I get home, I go into the moon room (what my grandmother and I call the bedroom we share), and I take the small glass with flowers that sits underneath the wooden Virgin. I throw yesterday's flowers into the trash can, put the two yellow roses in the little glass, and fill it with water. I then take the flowers and present them to the Virgin. Although my grandmother has me cut flowers from our garden for the Virgin every day, I don't think she has ever had such nice flowers as these. I'm hoping that these extra nice flowers will make the Virgin bring my grandmother back to me today.

My grandmother calls her Virgin the "Virgin of Guadalupe." She's wooden. She wears a blue wooden dress with gold stars, and a wooden gold crown on top of her head. She amazes me because she stands barefoot on top of a bunch of roses that have great big thorns. According to my grandmother, this particular Virgin appeared to a little Indian boy in the small Mexican town called Guadalupe. This is why she is called the "Virgin of Guadalupe." I have also heard my grandmother talk about the "Virgin of Fatima," and then there is a "Virgin of San Juan" in the church we go to in the town of San Juan, so I guess every town eventually gets its own Virgin.

After I dust the shelf where I put the flowers, I spend two hours moving my grandmother's bed by the two big open windows.

She always lets me put my bed by these windows so that I can keep my pickle jar with red ants on the windowsill and have my astronaut-moon-landing pictures on the wall above my bed. I know, though, that she really likes it best by the windows, too, since she likes to look out at the moon and hear the rain. Although she says she can still hear the rain from her side of the room, I know that she can't see the moon and that you hear the rain best up close to the windows.

While sweeping the moon room, I realize that the moon pictures are now on the wall on top of her bed and that the ants will be right by her face when she lies down. Although she likes my ants, I don't think she likes them so close by, especially now that she's so sick. I take the ants to the porch where they can get some sunlight. Then I proceed to take down my moon pictures, while standing on top of my grandmother's bed.

I know that my grandmother wouldn't mind having my twelve astronaut-moon-landing pictures staring down at her all the time, but I think she would prefer having her wooden crucifix on top of her bed, instead. She had let me take down her crucifix so that I could put up my moon pictures.

I get a free twelve-by-fifteen-inch picture from H.E.B., the supermarket, every week. I endure the weekly grocery shopping each Friday with my parents, just to be able to pick out the moon picture I want. I am always afraid that if I don't accompany my parents grocery shopping, they'll bring me back a moon picture I already have. I now only need three more moon pictures to have the whole collection. My grandmother's favorite moon picture is the one that has the astronaut in the white puffy suit floating in space. She likes this one best because it's my favorite one.

I put my twelve moon pictures in the drawer where she lets me keep my rocks, and then I take her crucifix and hang it over her bed. I notice while hanging her crucifix, though, that the wall is full of tiny holes. These holes are from the staples that had kept my moon pictures up. I sigh when I realize what I've done to my grandmother's wall, but I know that, when she sees it, she will just shake her head and smile.

When my mother finally pulls into the driveway after work, I run to her and ask her if my grandmother will come home today. She looks at me, shakes her head slowly, and then gives a heavy sigh. My grandmother is still very sick. I have to try to understand, she says, that my grandmother is very old—eighty-three—and that she has that disease where her bones break from the slightest thing. Her broken hip and ribs are healing, but very slowly, and the drugs she's taking for the pain are only making her delirious. My mother then tells me that when she went to visit my grandmother today, she had caught my grandmother grabbing crazily at the air with her hands. When my mother had asked her what she was doing, my grandmother told her that she was trying to catch the little white skeletons she saw flying through the air.

I tell my mother that my grandmother did not say that. She would never say anything as crazy as that, no matter how many strong drugs she was taking. I tear away from my mother's hug and run into the house.

I close the door to our bedroom which, I guess, we can no longer call the moon room, and sit on my grandmother's bed by the window. Her brown rocking chair is still empty. There are no smoke clouds from her Camel cigarette to watch curl and weave through the air. I wonder where I have to go to find the most beautiful flowers in the world for the Virgin, since apparently she doesn't think the yellow roses are nice enough.

At breakfast the next morning, I announce that I am going to visit my grandmother after school. My father just nods his head; my mother says that she'll leave work to drive me to the hospital. I tell her that I will walk there. It's not far. I know they're both wondering why all of a sudden I want to go visit my grandmother, since I have refused to go see her for the past two weeks, but they don't ask me any questions.

I dread going to see my grandmother because I don't want to see her anywhere but in our room, in her rocking chair. But I have to prove my mother wrong. My grandmother isn't grabbing at the air to catch skeletons. My grandmother has just been playing with my mother. She has just been trying to make her laugh. And if my grandmother had, in fact, seen the little skeletons and tried to catch them, then it would be our little secret — just hers and mine. I'll assure her that I'll tell my mother she had just been playing. She had just wanted to make my mother laugh.

I'll keep her secret, like she kept my secret the one night I brought my little dog in to sleep with me. There was a strict rule against bringing animals into the house. When my father asked my grandmother at breakfast if I had brought the dog in the night before, my grandmother sneaked a quick wink at my white, frozen face. Then she turned to him and told him no. I hadn't been able to stop coughing after hearing her response. My grandmother, who burned candles to the Virgin, gave her fresh flowers each and every day, and who prayed her rosary once in the morning and once at night, had outright lied to her very own son. My grandmother and I had later laughed about the incident in our moon room while eating orange candy slices (our favorite candy), and showing each other our orange teeth. She had me pick extra flowers for the Virgin that day.

I take the elevator to the fifth floor and walk into the room. I find a long, bony woman lying on a huge metal hospital bed. She is wrapped loosely in white sterile sheets. Her long white hair is all about her. Her back is towards the door, and with her thin long arm, she touches the gray partition that divides the small dark room. There are no windows in her narrow section. This old woman can't see the moon or hear the rain. She only whimpers in pain.

I know that if I walk down the hall only a little farther, I'll find my grandmother. She'll be rocking in her rocking chair. She'll be wearing her blue dress with the tiny squares, and her beautiful white hair will be made up in a little bun. She'll either be making white clouds with her cigarette or eating one of her orange candy slices. We'll laugh so hard together at the funny story she told my mother about the flying skeletons.

The woman with the long white hair turns to the door and catches my blur with her brown eye; her blue eye is blind. I come to her, and take her hand. She mumbles something, which I can't understand. She doesn't eat even one of the orange candy slices I give her. I leave when she starts talking about a coffee pot that she sees flying through the air.

I take the elevator down to the first floor of the hospital, and walk around the halls for twenty minutes until I find the desk where my mother works. I sit by her desk, and watch her shuffle papers and talk on the phone. When my mother asks about my visit with my grandmother, I look down at the floor, and tell her that my grandmother and I had a great time. We laughed and ate orange candy slices. I then tell her that I found out that my grandmother had made up the whole story about the flying skeletons. She had just wanted to make my mother laugh.

For that lie, I knew I would have to pick some extra flowers for the Virgin once I got home that day.

The Virgin

They emerged from her roof like smoke—first the heads, then their arms and trunks, and finally their legs. They took two, sometimes three small steps to the right, and then they leaped into the air, where they remained suspended for about three seconds before they finally vanished. They emerged from only one spot on her roof—one right after the other. There were at least a hundred of them, their strange shapes silhouetted against the moonlit sky. I had never seen anything like them before—skinny, about four feet tall, big ears. Instead of having flesh or fur, they were made of billions of tiny bright particles that bounced constantly against each other. The particles were light in color—purples, pinks, yellows, grays. Each one seemed to glow with its own inner light.

I wasn't scared as I watched the procession from my bedroom window. It was as my mother said it would be, except that the demons did not look like the red devil on the bingo cards. They didn't have horns or long tails. They weren't red, either. In the morning I would have to set her straight on the true appearance of demons.

I wondered, though, where my aunt had gotten the holy water, since she hadn't come with us to church. She had undoubtedly sprinkled her house with holy water. Why else would the demons be leaving? She must have had an old bottle of it stashed away some place. I wondered if there were as many demons leaving our house.

My mother had asked her to come with us to church,

but she had said she was going to watch the mass on TV. She didn't feel well. Her arthritis was acting up again. She was sure it would rain. I had asked my mother if I could also stay and watch the mass on TV, but she had said "no." It was a mortal sin not to go to church on Sunday. One would go directly to hell for such a sin. There wasn't even a short stop at purgatory. It was straight into the fire where ten devils beat you over the head with two-by-fours. However, according to my mother, my aunt didn't commit a mortal sin by not going since she was sick. Anyway, I should want to go to church today. We were going to get some holy water.

I had wanted to be sick, or even to be dying—anything to keep me from going to that church in San Juan. My parents loved to go to that church, which was at least a three-hour drive, because it had a Virgin who cured the sick, and made holy water.

The Virgin never moved—she didn't even blink. Every Sunday, for the entire ten hours of the mass, I watched her. I never took my eyes away from her. But I never saw her move. I couldn't understand how she cured people. Maybe she waited until everyone left the church before she climbed down from her glass box. She looked like a stupid doll to me—gold angel hair, bleached white face, huge blue glass eyes. If she moved at all, it was, indeed, with a great deal of effort, since she wore a purple velvet dress that seemed to weigh a ton. She wore this costume each and every Sunday. Maybe she never got dirty since she was so holy. But I couldn't see how she could stand to wear that thick dress during the hot summer months—even if she was so holy.

However much I believed that my parents drove all the way to San Juan for nothing, since the Virgin was really just a doll, the evidence was stacked heavily against me. She had medals and candles to prove that she had, indeed, cured many, many people. On each of her outstretched arms, she held about a million little medals hung on pieces of red, orange, and white string. They were in the shapes of legs, arms, heads—even eyes. My mother told me that people thanked the Virgin by giving her a medal in the shape of the part of the body that she had cured. But there couldn't possibly be that many arms and legs and eyes in the valley—or even in the whole world. The only way I could figure it out was that some people gave her five, or even ten arms, legs, or eyes, if they were really grateful.

Not only did they give her medals, but they walked on their knees all the way from the entrance of the church to the altar to give her their lit candles, which they put either in a tall baby blue or pink glass. It was at least a whole mile to the altar. All the way there, the people said their "Our Fathers" and "Hail Marys" so quickly that all you heard was a loud hum. One Sunday I tried counting all the Virgin's candles, which carpeted the floor below her, but I only managed to count up to nineteen. I knew, though, that she had more than a million of them—all glowing pink and blue.

Besides curing people, she also made holy water. After mass, my father filled an empty milk bottle with some of it. I carried it on my lap all the way home. It didn't look any different from ordinary drinking water, but who was I to question someone who had millions of medals and candles to prove her holiness? According to my mother, sprinkling this water all over our house would chase away all the evil demons. When I asked her what these demons looked like, she told me that they looked like the red devil on the bingo cards we bought in Mexico.

My father went from room to room sprinkling the water—the holy water—under the beds, on the walls, even inside my little closet. My mother followed closely behind him, mumbling "Our Fathers" and "Hail Marys" without pausing to breathe. I trailed behind them, watching as the drops of water fell first here, and then there. But not once did I see even the shadow of one little demon. My mother told me they would leave eventually. It would only be a matter of hours.

When I told them that morning that our house was cured of demons, since I had seen them leave Aunt Tala's house, they didn't believe me. Not even my mother believed me. She didn't come right out and say so, but from her queer look, I knew she didn't believe me.

That very next Sunday, I woke up early, and took the cigar box with my crayons and colored pencils from the shelf. With an orange-colored pencil, I drew a little demon like the ones I had seen. It was about three inches high. I drew it again. Three inches was too big. It had to be no bigger than an inch to be the size of her other medals. I cut it out, poked a tiny hole on the top of it, and through it, slipped a piece of red thread. I then tied the two ends of the string together to form a loop.

Throughout the mass, I stared at her, and at her medals. The longer I looked at her shiny medals, the more and more I realized that I couldn't give her my medal. All her medals were either gold or silver. Mine was only paper.

When the straw basket glided past me on its long thin wooden handle, I put my hand in it, and then withdrew it, still clutching the shiny quarter my mother had given me for the offering. While my parents lost themselves in conversation with some lady, I made my way to the altar. I dropped the quarter into an iron box, took one of the long narrow sticks, and lit a small burgundy candle that stood on the black metal stand below her.

The Magi

It is Christmas, a Mexican Christmas: There is hot, sweet chocolate made from melted squares of *Ibarra*, served in clay mugs with cinnamon sticks. There are piles of freshly made *sopapillas*—three-pointed puffy pillows, dipped in bowls of golden honey. There are thick red-white-striped peppermint sticks that soon turn chalk white and crunch cleanly when bitten. And then there is the tree, the Christmas tree, with the thin Mexican tin ornaments: angels, stars, birds, even a Santa Claus wearing a sombrero and riding a burro. The lights on the tree sparkle like brilliant December stars.

She sits there with her long white hair pulled back in a little bun. Her eyes look as small as dimes. She rocks to and fro in her brown plastic rocking chair. But ever so slowly now. She has a yellow dress on. The dress is made of sponge material, and it fits her stiffly, like the clothes on a scarecrow. I know it was given to her by one of the relatives. Her own clothes are thin cotton, with little holes from the Camel cigarettes she always puffs on. It is not that my grandmother has no new clothes. She has piles and piles of them, all sealed in plastic wrap and folded into perfect little squares. They are all given to her by relatives on her birthday or Christmas or some other holiday, but my grandmother never wears them. When relatives ask, she always says she is saving them for a special occasion.

When I see her wearing the yellow sponge dress, I know relatives have put her into it. I have never seen my grandmother in yellow, or, for that matter, in any other color but blue. Her own clothes are blue, all blue, like the sea, like the sky, like her blind eye. The sponge dress has no little holes. I notice her ashtray is gone from her side table. My grandmother rocks so slowly now, her rocking chair hardly moves.

My grandmother unexpectedly rises carefully and takes me to the Christmas tree. She lowers herself down on the floor beside me like an Indian and begins to whisper the story about the little barn under the tree. I am immediately drawn to the little grey donkey with the big eyelashes. But she makes me put the donkey down and turn my attention to a little brown baby that she carefully pulls out of her right dress pocket. She places the baby most carefully in the middle of my two cupped hands. I have no interest in the baby. I want to grab the donkey and make it gallop all around the Christmas tree and then have it nibble at a tree branch or two. I also want to tie a piece of kite string around its neck and hang it on the tree as an ornament. But then my grandmother whispers in my ear that I am holding a miracle in my hands. I don't know what this means, but when she says that a miracle is like an angel, I hold the baby most sacredly.

My grandmother says the baby was born on Christmas and that Christmas is when we celebrate his birthday. Since today is Christmas, I can now lay the baby in the wooden box in the barn. I ask her whether I should also put my red-and-white plastic Santa Claus on top of the roof of the barn. My grandmother thinks for a while, and then says that Santa Claus is a saint, which is also like an angel, but not as special as the baby. My grandmother lets me hang the plastic Santa Claus on the tree with a piece of kite string.

My grandmother then takes me to her chest of drawers. She opens the left top drawer and pulls out a small white cardboard box. From the box, she pulls out three round balls of white tissue paper. She takes one of the tissue balls and unravels it. There is a tall man in a fancy dress with a towel on his head and a box in his hands. Two other men in even fancier dresses emerge from the two other tissue balls, each with a box in his hands.

These are the three Magi, she says, the three kings. They are all carrying gifts to give to the baby. I ask her whether I can put them in the barn with the baby. She says not until the "pit or something" on the sixth of January. She says that is when they will finally arrive to see the baby from faraway. I ask my grandmother why the three tall kings in fancy dresses are traveling so far to see a little baby in straw. She says that, although the three kings are special, the baby is actually more special than even an angel.

In the end, I am able to talk my grandmother into putting the three men in dresses on her chest of drawers. And each day closer to the sixth of January, we walk them closer and closer to the baby in straw. One day I have to explain this arrangement to my mother when she wakes to find the three men in dresses on top of the kitchen sink, the halfway mark to the barn.

My grandmother's Christmas gift to me is a shiny silver dollar that has a picture of an angel with a circle of stars above her. My grandmother tells me to keep it in a secret place, and to take it out and look at the angel and stars when I feel sad. Like the Magi who arrive several days after Christmas with gifts for the baby, good things will come to make me feel better.

It takes forever to find my gift for her. I tell my mother I have to get my grandmother something really special. My mother takes me to Sears, to Penney's, to Woolworth's. She shows me handkerchiefs, slippers, scarfs.

I finally find it, on Christmas Eve, in the alley. It is a bit dusty and a bit bent. It is the best. It is blue and green and brown. It spins, sort of. It is the world.

I take the world home in a brown paper bag so my grandmother won't peek. Once home, I lock myself in the bathroom, the only room in the house that locks. I give the world a bath. I open a small bottle of red nail polish, the only color I can find, and paint in the chipped places on the world. I stick blue pins into it. I put the world in a box, wrap it in red Christmas paper, and tie a ribbon on it made from the twenty silver stick gum wrappers I've saved for just this purpose.

On the day of the epiphany, my grandmother finally opens her gift. She had let me open mine on Christmas day since I had not been able to wait. Her eyes get as big as silver dollars when she finally manages to pull the world out of its box. She gives a great laugh, a laugh that rings like a church bell on a cold December night.

What a magical gift, she says, beaming. What are all these blue pins? There must be hundreds of them.

I tell her that they mark all the places she and I are going to visit together. And that we are going to go by jet, ship, balloon, and, best of all, by horse. She leans back on her rocking chair and gives another great laugh. She then hands me her thick glasses so that I can look at these places as I would with a magnifying glass. We laugh together when I say that now she will have the special occasion to wear all those new clothes that relatives gave her.

The next time I see my grandmother she wears something new. It is a green, stiff dress. There is no rocking chair, just a wooden box, where she has been laid. There is a silver coin on each of her eyes, now closed.

❀ ❀ ❀

I take the silver dollar out of my right blue dress pocket. I look at the angel, the stars. I know only then that the Magi have arrived, and that they have added blue pins to the sky.

The Carousel

"Father Francisco came by today," my grandmother muses. "The church *jamaica*, that's what he came to talk to me about. Needs to raise money to fix the roof. It's getting so that more and more people are coming to mass. But not for his sermons. No, they come to see what the wind will blow off the altar he always likes to hide behind. It's becoming an insult to the Lord, he says. Two Sundays ago, at the early mass, the wind came at such an angle it sent that gold cup of his flying. White hosts went everywhere. One even hit Mrs. Gómez in the eye. All the congregation stood stunned. They had no idea what to do. Should they help him pick up the hosts? But they are holy, and they had been instructed never to touch one. So they just stood there, paralyzed. Some had hosts stuck to their hair, their coats. It was a mess. Father Francisco spent a whole hour finding all the hosts and putting them back into that gold cup. It was no wonder, given where the hosts wound up, that no one went to take communion."

"So what does he want you to do?" I ask.

"Oh, help out in some way. Maybe make and sell tamales or *menudo* at the *jamaica*. But, given what a *jamaica* makes, the Father is not going to get his new roof. This is not good since stories are getting up to the bishop that Father Francisco is not doing a good job here. The incident of the flying hosts. Well, as the Father's luck would have it, someone from the paper was there and he

15

wrote a story about what had happened. But the reporter, not knowing that it was because of the bad roof, said that Father Francisco had gotten so fat, 'rotund' was the word he used, that he no longer fit on the altar, and that he was knocking over everything with his great big behind."

"Well, Father Francisco is kind of fat, don't you think?"

"The Father is fat, but Fathers are supposed to be fat. When you have a congregation like ours, here, well you're going to get fat, what with everyone inviting you here and there for a few *taquitos,* a little bowl of *menudo,* a tiny cup of chocolate with a thin slice of cake. You can't say no. Anyway, the Father needs a roof now. We'll put him on a diet later."

My grandmother tells me to put my shoes on. We are going over to see Pepino. I always like to go visit Pepino. He lives in a place full of treasures. I don't know why they call it a junkyard.

When we get to Pepino's place, we find him inside one of the old cars in his lot. The car has no tires, no windows. Pepino is unscrewing the steering wheel. He bangs his head when we finally catch his attention. He greets us with a big smile. His teeth are green. This is why his name is Pepino.

My grandmother asks Pepino about the carnival that had been in town last year, whether the carnival people had left anything behind. Pepino squints his eyes, which seems to make him remember better.

"Well, a couple of old tires, a broken cage where one of the tigers went," he said.

"Anything else?"

"Well, no, oh, yeah, there was the rusty carousel, now junk. The thing is a mess. Rust everywhere. And the horses, the carousel horses, they are rotten through. The thing no longer worked, so they just left it, abandoned it. I brought it over to use for scrap."

My grandmother asks to see it. We walk past old stoves, refrigerators with no doors, crooked ironing boards, rusty bathtubs, and other great places for hide-and-seek. In the far end of the lot, sits the carousel. Just rusted metal. The carousel horses have no heads. They are missing legs, tails. They are so rotten no one can even sit on them anymore.

My grandmother circles the carousel. She then tells Pepino about the *jamaica*. She asks for the carousel. Pepino says that even he thinks the carousel is junk, useless. But, well, if my grandmother wants it for the jamaica, to go ahead, she can have it.

Our next stop is at Julio's. Julio is the town's *santero*. He carves saints out of wood. We find Julio outside his house, sitting on a treetrunk. His hands move deftly over the emerging face of what he says will be Saint Anthony. "See, Señora Marta, lost her wedding ring. In hysterics. A few prayers to Saint Anthony, and that should do it."

My grandmother tells Julio about the *jamaica*, about the roof, about the carousel. My grandmother asks Julio whether he can help. He asks how. She asks him whether he can carve out a few carousel horses. Julio falls off the trunk.

"I carve only saints, only saints. No horses, no, just saints," he stutters.

We leave.

During the month after Father Francisco's visit, the Father gains twenty pounds. He visits my grandmother and tells her how worried he is that the *jamaica* will not raise enough money for the new roof. He asks my grandmother whether she has anything to go with the tea she gives him. My grandmother offers him an apple. The Father looks at the apple as though he were being offered a brick. My grandmother then notes that he must not be very hungry, or, otherwise, he wouldn't be so particular.

Three days before the *jamaica*, my grandmother and I head over to Pepino's. We find him tinkering with the inside workings of the carousel.

"No," he says, "it's useless. It will never move, revolve."

Pepino, nevertheless, agrees to drag the rusty carousel over to the *jamaica* grounds tomorrow with his truck.

The night before the *jamaica*, I find my grandmother in the kitchen preparing *café de olla*, a very special coffee made with cinnamon water and sweetened with *piloncillo*. She carefully pours the *café de olla* into her silver thermos, making sure not a drop is spilled. When my grandmother says we are going over to the *jamaica* grounds, I tell her I do not understand why. It is a waste of time. She will just be embarrassed because the carousel is dirt. She looks at me and hands me the silver thermos to carry.

When we get there we find Pepino. He is unloading the carousel. He has given it a fresh coat of yellow paint, with drawings of clouds, angels, and winged horses in greens, pinks, and blues. Next a white pickup truck pulls up. It is Julio. The back of the truck is covered with white blankets. We help Julio unload seven objects from the back of the truck. Each is carefully wrapped in a white sheet. Julio unwraps the first object. We stare in amazement. It is Saint Anthony, and he is riding a red horse. The next is Saint Cecilia on a blue camel. Then out pops Saint Theresa on a pink lion, Saint Joseph on a striped purple-and-yellow ostrich, and last, the Virgin Mary, on a great big green giraffe.

"Well, I told you I only do saints," Julio says with a funny smile. My grandmother pours Pepino and Julio a cup of hot *café de olla*.

The next day, the line is a mile long. Young and old alike stand in line to ride with the Virgin Mary or their favorite saint on the carousel. Father Francisco makes each new set of carousel riders go round and round by circling the carousel five times in his dusty red tennis shoes. And each time the Father passes by, each rider tries to get a free ride by trying to grab the long peacock feather that he wears stuck to his blue baseball cap.

After this, a story comes out in the paper, from the same reporter as before, saying that his earlier story had apparently done the job since Father Francisco had become "Slimmy the Jimmy" and mass was now back to normal in the little church with a brand-new roof.

Nopalitos

When I kneel beside my grandmother in front of a coffin to pay my last respects to Doña Tomacita, I am startled to find a large black frying pan on top of Doña Tomacita's rather round stomach. She has little red lips and two red dots, one on each cheek. Never before had I seen any makeup on Doña Tomacita's face, just streaks of gravy and salsa — whatever she was cooking, and she was always cooking.

I remember one early morning in March I heard loud honking outside. It was Doña Tomacita. She was in her rusty, rattling, gray 1950 Chevrolet truck, which she called Josephina, after Napoleon's wife. My grandmother and I ran outside. My grandmother carried a large straw basket with one arm and a bundle of old newspapers under the other. She climbed up front with Doña Tomacita; I went in the bed of the truck with the basket. I liked it best back there. I bounced up and down, and got whipped by the wind. My long hair flew out like a great blazing fire. I held on tightly to the basket, while I sat on the bundle of newspapers. I wondered where Doña Tomacita was taking us this time.

We drove for about an hour, dodging cars, poles, dogs, two large tumbleweeds, and a red chicken. Doña Tomacita was the very worst driver in town. She had no driver's license, although she had taken the test forty-three times. My grandmother and I had become famous in town since we were Doña Tomacita's only willing passengers. My grandmother and I didn't worry one bit about her driving since, according to my grand-mother, Saint Christopher helped her drive. Saint Christopher stood front and center, about a foot high, on Josephina's dashboard. I often thought that Doña Tomacita's mad driving was partly due to not being able to see clearly with that big saint blocking the windshield. But then, how else could it be that Doña Tomacita hadn't killed herself and mown down half the town's popula-tion? Yet I wished Saint Christopher would take a driv-ing lesson or two. We suddenly turned off the road onto a dirt road, where the bouncing got serious, even better than a roller-coaster ride, then up a hill, where I had to hold on tight to the side of the truck because there was no tailgate to keep me from sliding off completely. Then, boom, a dead halt. I bounced three feet into the air and landed on my feet.

Doña Tomacita leaped out of Josephina. She was full of excitement. I wondered what she was pointing to since all I saw were three tall cactus trees behind a barbed-wire fence. I spotted a green bird and four spar-rows. The ground was lively with silver lizards. I won-dered whether Doña Tomacita was excited about the birds, or lizards, and whether we were going to catch some and put them in the basket.

They explained to me that my job was to carry the big basket and the old newspapers. My grandmother and Doña Tomacita armed themselves with big shiny knives. I looked around to see what they planned to kill with those big knives of theirs. I saw nothing, just more birds and lizards.

I followed them to the barbed-wire fence. We helped each other through the fence. I was the only one to get stuck. I pulled, but my T-shirt was hooked on a barb. I gave my T-shirt a strong yank. It tore. I fell to the ground and immediately jumped to my feet. I quickly looked around. Nothing. I now feared that Doña Tomacita and my grandmother were after something invisible — a witch, perhaps. I remembered hearing that, if you saw a green light in the sky, it was really a witch, and that, if you said an "Our Father" backwards, the light would turn into a witch and fall to the ground in flames. I looked at the sky. No flying green lights.

Doña Tomacita and my grandmother quietly walked through the brush and approached the three cactus trees. They circled the trees, examining them. The cactus trees were full of brand-new light green paddles that looked like heads. Each head was covered with about a hundred thorns. Doña Tomacita smiled. I wondered why she smiled.

They took out gloves and put them on. I put on a pair of green gloves my grandmother handed me. The fingers of the gloves were two inches too long. They told me to place the big straw basket on the ground next to the middle cactus tree. The basket reached up to my waist. They motioned for me to place the bundle of old newspapers next to the basket, which I did.

Doña Tomacita and my grandmother took the shiny long knives in their right hands. They were positioned to attack. I quickly looked around to see if I saw something suspicious. I saw nothing. I turned back to them. They quietly approached the middle cactus tree.

I watched. My grandmother and Doña Tomacita took hold of a new cactus head with their left hands. With their right, they took the sharp knife and cut along the line where the head connected to the cactus tree. Then they explained my job. I placed a sheet of newspaper at the bottom of the basket. Each head was then placed on the newspaper, side by side. Once the newspaper was covered with one layer, I placed another sheet of newspaper on top of that layer. My grandmother and Doña Tomacita then filled that piece of newspaper with another single layer of heads. This process went on and on. Each layer of heads did not tangle up with the next. You didn't want the thorns to stick all the heads together into a big, thorny green ball. We worked one cactus tree, then another. The basket was full after harvesting all three. I wondered whether they were cutting up a witch that had transformed itself into a cactus tree or whether Doña Tomacita was planning to grow a big forest of cactus trees by planting the heads in the dirt around her house. If the latter, I wondered why not plant trees that didn't have thorns and could give shade. Trees that could support a swing and be climbed. If the former, I wondered if the witch was now dead or if it might rematerialize and jump me.

We returned to the truck. Both my grandmother and Doña Tomacita helped me with the basket. I asked whether I could ride in front with them. They said I needed to keep the basket steady in the back.

Before I hopped onto the truck, they asked me to find three rocks with lots of edges. It took me ten minutes to find them. I wondered what the rocks were for. Perhaps to plant the heads somehow. Perhaps to throw at the witch if it tried to pop out of the basket.

We headed back. I sat in the corner of the truck, steadying the basket with my feet. I kept my gloves on, one rock in each hand. The third rock I put on top of the basket. I kept my eyes on the basket and watched for any witch signs.

After what seemed like hours, we arrived at Doña Tomacita's house. I was relieved when my grandmother and Doña Tomacita appeared to help unload the basket. We took the basket to the front cement porch. Doña Tomacita set out three pieces of newspaper on the cement floor, each with one of the rocks I found and a small knife.

Doña Tomacita and my grandmother sat themselves in front of one of the newspapers. They put their gloves back on. I watched as each one took a tender head out of the basket, placing it on the piece of newspaper in front of her. Holding each head by the edge, they carved off a thorn by cutting around it with the sharp little knife. They cleaned the thorn off the knife by scraping against the rock. They took off another thorn and then another until the head was perfectly clean of all thorns. Then each one took another head out of the basket and did the same.

After Doña Tomacita and my grandmother finished cleaning ten *nopalitos* each, they turned to me. They said that it was time for me to try one. I was nervous. I didn't want to get stuck with thorns or get cut with the knife or touch a part of a witch. Doña Tomacita read me. I said that they were wasting their time taking the thorns off the heads since they would grow just fine if they planted them with the thorns on. Doña Tomacita squinted her eyes.

"These are *nopalitos*," she said. "Removing the thorns off the nopalitos is like removing the thorns off Christ's head."

Now I was really confused. I thought they were carving a witch or preparing the heads to plant in the ground. Perhaps, I thought, it had something to do with Lent. We were in the middle of Lent then. I always knew it was Lent because my grandmother told me I had to give up what I really liked best until Easter. I always tried to give up eating candy since I liked candy best, but I always wound up sneaking it at night or when no one was watching. And I was never swallowed up by the earth or struck dead by a big lightning bolt. In other words, Lent didn't make any sense, and this didn't either.

But I was still nervous. As far as I knew, Christ had only one head, and there must have been at least a hundred cactus heads in the basket. I wasn't nervous about getting stuck with thorns or cut with the knife anymore. I was nervous about doing this holy thing with Christ and the thorns right. I remembered hearing how some people in the Bible turned to stone—or was it salt?—for just looking back or something simple like that.

I carefully selected a small, little head. After ten minutes of work and concentration, I managed to cut one thorn off successfully. On the second thorn, I cut too deeply. I was terrified, wondering whether this meant that I just cut Christ in half. My grandmother and Doña Tomacita, each now on their fifteenth one, stopped. They looked at me and then at the head I sliced in half. They asked me to bring them some ice water. Perhaps they were going to try to piece the head together. I prayed I wouldn't turn into a rock.

I ran inside Doña Tomacita's house and put some ice and water into a tall green glass. I ran outside and handed Doña Tomacita the glass of ice water. I stepped back. Doña Tomacita took the glass, looked at it, drank it down, and then burped. My grandmother laughed. Doña Tomacita laughed. She told me that God was laughing and to try again.

I tried again. By the time I finally finished one half of the cactus head I sliced in half, they had finished with the entire basket. My grandmother and Doña Tomacita waited patiently until I finished the other half of the *nopalito*. They said I had done a nice job. The clean *nopalitos* were placed in a shiny metal bucket.

We followed Doña Tomacita into her house with the bucket. Doña Tomacita had us sit down at her little wooden kitchen table by the open window.

Doña Tomacita then seemed to go into a trance. She washed the *nopalitos* in cold water. She opened a drawer and pulled out a long knife. She reached into the metal bucket and pulled out a head to place onto a wooden board. She took the knife and cut into the head. She made five slices lengthwise and five widthwise. She put the thin rectangles she created into a bowl. She took out a second head and did the same. She did the same to all the heads in the bucket. Then put a large black frying pan on the stove. Once the pan was red hot, she poured the *nopalitos* into the skillet and stirred with a wooden spoon. The *nopalitos* spat and sizzled.

There was a knock on the door. It was Doña Martínez and her eight children. I had seen Don Martínez the week before. He had looked blue and bloated in his coffin. I helped place a folding table next to the small kitchen table. A white bed sheet was draped over the two connected tables. The table was set with plates, cups, paper napkins, plastic forks and spoons. Doña Tomacita stepped outside and returned with a handful of yellow wildflowers and a beautiful white Easter lily. She put water into an empty jar, filled it with the flowers, and placed them at the center of the table.

Doña Tomacita called everyone to the table. She presented a big white bowl heaped with the sizzling hot *nopalitos*. There was a small bowl of *guajillo* salsa and another one with a batch of refried beans. Hot corn tortillas were stacked high inside a straw basket covered with an embroidered white cotton cloth to keep them hot. There was hot coffee and cold fresh milk.

Doña Tomacita finally took a seat at the table. Then the octopus dance began: arms, hands went every which way, making tacos, passing the *nopalitos*, the refried beans, the hot salsa, pouring hot coffee, the cold milk. Everyone was talking and eating. The faces of the Martínez family finally smiled. Doña Tomacita, whose mouth was streaked with red salsa, smiled.

❀ ❀ ❀

When I ask my grandmother why they put a frying pan in with Doña Tomacita, my grandmother quietly turns and whispers two words to me, "*Nopalitos*, remember?"

The Tiny Bubble

When my cousin Glenda phones and says to come over, I know she has a secret to tell me. She always tells me secrets at her house. My house is not good for telling secrets because my two brothers and little sister are always popping around, wanting to know everything. Because Glenda has no siblings and because her mother is always working, her house is perfect for telling secrets. I wonder, though, why Glenda isn't giggling when she calls. She always giggles when she has a secret to tell me.

I don't want to hear her secret when I see her face through the screen door. She looks weird, like she's embarrassed or something. I don't want to go inside, but I do because she looks serious. Glenda (I call her "Go" because she calls me "Bo") only looks serious when her latest cat dies or when she is mad at me. So she must be mad at me because I just saw her cat, Frisky, alive and well. She was sleeping on the damp ground under the ebony tree.

As I follow her into the kitchen, I try to remember what I did to make her mad this time. We watched "Boo" on TV last night at her house. She was not mad at me then because we had both laughed at the monster. He wasn't scary: He was a giant big eye with scales and six skinny legs. We had also tried out one of the secrets she learned from someone at school, which was to drop a small bag of Planter's salted peanuts into a bottle of cold Dr. Pepper and then to pop it quickly into our mouths while the soda fizzed up. This secret made us both happy because no one in our neighborhood knew about this combination. I didn't like the taste of the wet peanuts and the salty soda water, but, of course, I didn't tell her that. The important thing was that we had a secret no one else knew about. We could go around telling everybody that we had a secret, which made us feel special, like we had created a little world of our own.

Glenda sits at the table and tells me to sit in the chair next to her. I want to sit in the chair farthest away from her, but I don't argue because I feel she's mad enough, already. She then makes me more uncomfortable. She takes the little glass salt shaker with the silver top, and starts moving it around and around in circles on top of the wooden table. It makes a scraping sound, which I feel inside. Her eyes follow the orbiting salt shaker; I follow her eyes. You would think I had eaten her cat, she looks so serious.

With her eyes still on the salt shaker, she says that she has a secret to tell me. It's not a fun secret, she adds. She tells me that my mother asked her to tell me this secret. I don't have time to wonder what secret my mother couldn't tell me herself, because all of a sudden I watch Go's hands curl into index fingers. They land on her head. One points to the top of her head, the other to her forehead.

With her index fingers pointing at her head like guns, Go takes a breath, and with a cracking voice, says that all girls have a tiny bubble inside their heads, located somewhere between her two index fingers. After taking another breath, she squeaks that, as one gets older, the tiny bubble travels down through the body. The index finger pointed at her forehead starts traveling down the bridge of the her nose, over her mouth, chin, neck, and chest. It stops at her stomach. Now the salt shaker starts orbiting again. With the help of yet another breath, she says that the tiny bubble pops when a girl gets to be twelve or thirteen. Now the salt shaker is spinning so fast it could take off on its own. When the tiny bubble pops, she continues, blood comes out of it, and it leaves the body from "down there."

Although she lost me the moment she pointed her index fingers like guns to her head, I ask her what she means by "down there." She only gives me an embarrassed look and repeats that the blood comes from "down there." I ask her if "down there" is one's toes, but she just makes her eyes white by turning them inside her head. I want to continue asking what she means by "down there," but I feel that, if I ask her one more question about "down there," her big head will pop and the blood making her look like a big red tomato will come out from "up there."

I decide to ask if the tiny bubble inside her head has popped, instead. I should never have asked this question. I thought it was a good question. She is twelve, almost thirteen. She just finished telling me that the tiny bubble pops at the age of twelve or thirteen. But now she is really mad at me. She leaves her chair abruptly, telling me that she needs to tell me more—some other time, though. I am sorry I made her mad, but at least now I can leave her uncomfortable house with the orbiting salt shaker and return to my cartoons.

I nod when my mother asks me if Glenda has talked to me. I want to tell her that I don't understand her secret and to ask her why she couldn't tell me her secret, herself. But I don't dare ask her any questions, because she looks like Go—embarrassed.

Finally, a cartoon explains what "down there" means. We watch it in the school cafeteria, while the boys play kickball outside. I just knew we were going to learn about the tiny bubble that pops, when I saw the same embarrassed look on the P.E. teacher that I had seen on my mother and on Go. As we squirm on the cold metal folding chairs, the film talks with the voice of a fairy godmother. The film has a transparent, cartoon body of a girl with a cartoon brain and a "V" on her cartoon stomach.

The "V" has a little circle on each side. The nice cartoon colors of her insides — pinks, light blues, yellows — go well with the fairy godmother's voice.

When the fairy godmother starts talking about a little bubble in the cartoon brain called the pituitary, I know this is the tiny bubble Go was trying to tell me about. As I listen further to the fairy godmother, I realize that Go told me the story all wrong. The tiny bubble never leaves the brain to travel down the body. It sends a messenger, called a hormone, instead. The messenger sails through the body until it reaches one of the circles on the side of the "V." Once there, the messenger wakes up one of the little eggs that sleep in the circle and sends it down the "V." The little egg floats until it gets stuck inside the "V" with paste or something. When the egg ripens, it falls from the "V." It then leaves the body in a little pool of blood.

When I finally realize what "down there" means from the cartoon, I feel embarrassed, and then angry. I feel angrier when the embarrassed teacher pulls out a small white pillow from a blue box with a white flower. She tells us we can catch the pool of blood on the silly pillow. I wonder how, but I don't ask. She then tries to hang the pillow on a white elastic band. By then, none of us watch, much less listen. When the teacher tries to pass around her silly pillow contraption and a few of her silly pillows, we throw them up in the air and at each other.

When one of the boys asks our homeroom teacher if they will see a film like the girls just did, the teacher just smirks, and then shakes his head. I feel angry again. It seems so unfair. We have to wear silly pillows; the boys don't. I then wonder if these pillows will make you float or sink when you go swimming.

I pray for the tiny ball in my head never to pop. But it pops one day. I tell myself to laugh. But I can't laugh. I just feel embarrassed, and then angry. I use cotton. The red cotton I wrap in layers of newspaper and secretly throw in the trash can outside. I am determined to keep this a secret. I don't want to make others feel embarrassed.

I feel angriest when my mother discovers my secret. She finds red clothes when sorting clothes to wash. She tries to talk to me, but I just want to be alone. I don't feel comfortable in my body anymore, much less with other people.

She takes a pencil and a piece of paper. She writes down a word that begins with the letter "K." She tells me to give the word to Rita at the corner grocery store, and not to give it to her husband, who also works there. I don't want to go, but I feel I have no choice, just as I have no choice over what my body is doing on its own.

When I give the word to Rita, she looks embarrassed. I want to tell her the box is not for me, that it is for my mother. But I know she knows the box is for me. When she takes the blue box with the white flower from the shelf, her husband walks in. He looks at the box, and then at me. I look away. I don't want to see him smirk. Rita puts the blue box with the white flower in a large brown bag, although she didn't put the box of Corn-flakes I bought that morning in a paper bag.

I tell my mother I will not use a silly contraption. She uses two safety pins, instead. I finally go to sleep knowing I won't go swimming tomorrow and that everyone will wonder why.

I wake up twelve years later, and ask my mother about the tiny bubble that popped. I ask her why she could not tell me, why she made me feel embarrassed. She squints her eyes and says she doesn't know. She then tells me that she had never been told as a young woman, and that when her bubble popped, she honestly thought she was dying.

The Egg

The cold white egg goes around and around my eyes in a figure eight. I count the full cycles each time the egg crosses the bridge of my nose.

A large woman, all in white, looms above me like some great spirit. She moves the egg as if it's a magical stone, given to her by some wizard to cure the sick and foretell the future. My mother stands silently by the doorway, moving her lips as she softly prays along with the stranger. One "Hail Mary" ends and, without pause, another begins. An "Our Father" follows a string of "Hail Marys." As the ceremony continues, the words blur. All I hear is mumbling, a nasal hum. I wonder if she is even breathing. I wonder who she is. I wonder where my mother is. I pray silently for this to stop.

The doctors can't cure me. My eyes are killing me. My mother thinks I'm going blind.

My mother was taught as a child that if she liked another's, say, eyes or nose, she had to touch them; otherwise, the person's eyes or nose would be cursed. Perhaps someone had liked my eyes, she said; perhaps what she was taught as a child is just Mexican superstition, I said. Then a woman in white appeared at my bedroom door. She had a white egg in one hand and a white ceramic cup in the other.

Ninety, ninety-one . . . one hundred, the egg continues on its orbit, uninterrupted by the darkness that enters through the open window. The egg seems to acquire a strange glow, as if reflecting the light of the full moon outside. Unable to make out anything anymore, all I see is the glowing white egg.

I need this strangeness to stop. I need things to be normal once more. Pain is normal; an orbiting egg is not. My mother as my mother is normal; my mother as a wizard's assistant is not. I wonder how prayer seems normal with a church, but seems bizarre with an egg. An egg is to be cooked and eaten with salt. It's okay if eyes burn.

The egg stops. The humming stops, too. The egg then quickly departs from my head like a small white ghost.

I hear the egg. It is cracked and then poured into the cup. The cup is placed under the bed, directly under my head.

The next morning, I quickly open my eyes. The pain has vanished. There is no blur. I run and tell my mother. She runs to my bedroom and pulls the cup from under my bed. The orange round yolk is streaked blind with a blurry white cloud. My mother says it's the sign of the curse; I say nothing.

At breakfast that morning, I watch my sister's long hair glisten like copper with the brilliant sun.

As I carry my empty plate into the kitchen, I intentionally walk past my sister and discreetly touch her hair with the back of my left hand.

The Feather

It's taller than me, about five feet. It's the color of a white cloud, and it glows. I find it hanging from our ebony tree. It is stained with blue, the color of blue ink.

I take the feather inside to my grandmother. Her eyes grow wide upon seeing the feather. She examines it carefully. She then tells me that she doesn't know what it belongs to, where it came from.

She suggests I place the feather by my bed and ask the dream world for an answer. That night I place the feather next to me in bed, cover it with the blanket, and ask for an answer.

When I awaken the next morning, I sense my grandmother has been waiting for me to open my eyes.

"So what is the answer?" she asks.

I close my eyes to try to catch the flavors of any dreams I might have had before the morning sun quickly evaporates them. I yawn to buy time, to clear the fog in my mind. My grandmother continues to study my face.

"So you did dream it," she says.

I tell her I did not dream it, or at least, I did not dream anything that made any sense. There was a woman, a very young woman with loops and loops of braided hair. The woman was very dark in color. I don't know who the woman was.

"Oh, so you did dream it," she adds.

I look at her, still yawning, still not understanding. "What do you mean?" I ask.

She doesn't respond.

Then I reach and pull the feather out from under the covers. Its glow has become even more intense, as though it is alive and is radiating light from within. While washing my face, I look through the window and find my grandmother outside looking up at the sky and then at the ebony tree where I found the feather.

"The feather," I ask, through the window, "belongs to the young black woman I dreamt?" My grandmother just looks at me and then turns to look at the sky and the ebony tree, again.

"What would this woman be doing with such a feather? What would anybody be doing with such a feather?" I ask.

Her answer is the same: Ask the dream world. That night I dream about a silver plane. It crashes and loses a wing. I tell my grandmother about the dream, and that it doesn't make sense. She just nods.

I take two crayons, a black one and a white one. On a sheet of notebook paper, I draw, then color the young black woman as I dreamt her: white robe, black complexion, braided hair, blue eyes. I draw the feather on the side. After showing the drawing to my grandmother, I post it on the ebony tree with a tack.

Nothing happens the rest of the day. Wondering whether perhaps the wind might blow the drawing away, I take a flashlight and go to the ebony tree. The drawing is gone. I tell my grandmother. I ask her whether I should draw another one. She tells me to wait until tomorrow, that perhaps it was not the wind exactly that took the drawing away.

I awaken the next morning to a knock at the front door. I peek through the venetian blinds. I see a pair of red pumps with three-inch heels. The person wearing them is teetering in them.

My grandmother asks me who is knocking on the door. I tell her that all I see is a pair of high-heel shoes, red ones, the color of a fire engine. She asks me to go see who it is while she finishes dressing. I run out of the room in my yellow pajamas with feet and open the door a crack. Above the tall, fire-engine-red pumps, I see a great big white trench coat. Above that, a dark face with bright red lips. Above the red lips, two huge blue eyes and loops and loops of braided hair.

I open the door and stare. The trench coat looks very bulky around the shoulders and back. The fire-engine-red pumps keep moving up and down as though they are too tight, too big, or too high. The long red fingernails carry a white paper box tied with white string.

I am still staring when my grandmother comes to the door. She looks at the woman in the fire-engine-red pumps and motions for her to come in. The woman sits on the sofa. When my grandmother asks to hang her trench coat, the woman silently shakes her head no. When my grandmother goes out to make some tea, I notice that there is a large blue stain on the trench coat near her shoulder.

My grandmother returns with a pot of hot tea and three white cups. I return with the white feather. I take a seat on the other end of the sofa and place the feather between the visitor and me. I stand it up so that it leans against the back of the sofa.

My grandmother pours three cups of hot tea. I watch closely as the woman in the red high heels does precisely what my grandmother does: two teaspoons of white sugar, two teaspoons of white sugar, a splash of milk, a splash of milk, stir, stir. All the while the bulk on her shoulders under the trench coat keeps wiggling, and the blue ink spot keeps getting bigger and bigger.

The woman hands my grandmother the white cardboard box. My grandmother unties the string around the box and opens it. From the box she lifts a round fluffy white cake that looks as light as a feather. My grandmother disappears into the kitchen and comes back with a knife to cut the cake. Each of us has a slice of cake and two cups of tea. When we finish, the woman points to the cake and then to the pocket in her trench coat. My grandmother leaves the room and returns with a piece of wax paper. She takes the knife and cuts off a thick slice of cake, wraps it neatly in the piece of wax paper, and hands it to the woman. The woman takes it and slides it into her pocket.

The woman then raises herself carefully from the sofa. She turns to the feather and then turns to me. I turn to my grandmother. My grandmother nods. I pick it up and hand it to the woman. The woman smiles. She stumbles to the door as though she has never worn high heels in her life before. She smiles and nods when she gets to the door. At the door, she shakes my grandmother's hand and then my hand. When she turns to go through the door, the bulk of her shoulders hits the frame as though she is not used to walking through doorways. With feather in hand, she stumbles forth down the street in her fire-engine-red pumps.

When we can no longer see the woman in the distance, we return to the house. Neither of us says a word.

The next morning we hear on the radio that a child is found alive after being lost for three days. According to the newscaster, the child seems healthy, except for a bit of delirium. The child, strangely, keeps talking about a young black woman who fed her cake and kept her warm in her fluffy white wings. The child's white T-shirt was stained all over with what looks like blue ink. When asked about the blue stains, the little girl said that the angel was a bit clumsy. Then she said that all she wanted now was another slice of the angel's cake.

The Bubble Gum Pink House

One morning, Nata wakes up to find five people stretched out on white beach chairs on her front lawn, each wearing giant yellow plastic sunglasses, the type worn by circus clowns. When Nata goes out to ask what this is all about, they say they are merely there to witness, and to witness firsthand, the incredible bubble gum pink paint of her house, that it is such a psychedelic experience, really, that they need to wear their sunglasses, for, otherwise, they will damage their very sensitive eyes.

Nata, instantly turning bright pink herself, shoots back that it is she who should be wearing the sunglasses, what with the sun's glare from their big white thighs, and that if they don't get off her grass now, she is going to take her gun and spray paint them shocking pink to match her house. Not knowing how exactly to take Nata — given that she did paint her house a hideous bubble gum pink — they leap out of their beach chairs and flee, shouting that they are going to take this up with the mayor, just wait and see.

Then the papers come, rolled up like sacred scrolls, each placed at everyone's door, that is, everyone with a colorful house, at least one that isn't white, or beige, or grey, or, as Nata likes to say, the color of *animal muerto* (dead animal).

The color of the papers is, of course, white, and the papers read like declarations of war, proclaiming that those with houses painted in shocking, screaming colors are destroying the neighborhood, devaluing property values, and even creating a serious health hazard to people's eyes — like throwing raw alcohol into them.

Well, this gets Nata's blood boiling scarlet red, especially since it was just that morning that she had found those strange people lounging around on her front yard. That afternoon, after a shot of tequila for fortification and a quick kiss to her poster of Emiliano Zapata, the one she bought on sale for fifty cents, she heads out the door with a big sharpened pencil and a serious metal clipboard.

She starts with the purple house. She introduces herself when an elderly woman finally comes to the door. The elderly woman smiles when she learns that Nata lives in the pretty pink house nearby. As Nata finishes her second cup of hot Mexican chocolate, the elderly woman, named Marta, reveals that she initially was a little reluctant to open the door because she thought Nata was the one who had put the paper scroll at her door and was now there in person to complain about her purple house. Marta then goes on to say that purple is her favorite color, that it reminds her of the purple grapes that grew outside her bedroom window as a child. She loved watching the birds come to eat the little grapes. There were so many of them — blue ones, green ones, yellow ones, and sometimes, even red ones. She also loved eating them herself, rolling the cool marbles around her mouth, tasting their bursting sweetness.

She remembers when she was finally able to buy her little house, after more than thirty years of working as a maid, a dishwasher, a cook, after saving every coin, disciplining herself to only two meals a day, sometimes going without heat, medicine. The very first thing she did, once the house was officially in her name, was to go out and buy several cans of paint. She had then carefully painted her house from top to bottom, the color of purple grapes. It was her happiest day ever. It made her feel close to her childhood memories of the grapevines. It also made her feel proud, genuinely proud, of finally owning something of her very own. She was somebody now, and not just a maid, or a "Mexican," or a "wetback," as she sometimes heard herself described in whispers. Painting her house purple was her way of announcing to the world, to everyone, and especially to herself, that she was not invisible anymore, that she was Marta, someone very much alive—bright purple!—in fact. And now no one could ever claim again not to notice her, not even in the dark.

Nata says that the color of her pink house is the color of the seashells she found and collected as a girl in her little fishing village in Mexico. She loved the sea-salt smell of the pink seashells and the soothing sound of the sea she heard echoing from inside them.

They then discuss the paper scroll, the declaration of war. Marta then joins Nata, and they walk over to the orange house on the next block, each carrying her paper scroll like a sword. The evening is falling, and the red hibiscus, the purple *jacarandas,* and the bright yellow roses give off the rays of sun collected all day, in a mist of brilliant, luminous colors.

Nata knocks on the orange door, and a tall, dark-eyed man in an orange flannel shirt comes to the door. Before they even announce they are Nata and Marta, they say that they come from the pink and purple houses across the way and that they really like his bright orange house. Paco, as it turns out, gives a sigh of relief and then fetches them each a glass of freshly squeezed orange juice.

They ask him what he thinks about the paper, the scroll. He hesitates, and then says that he is quite confused by it, that he can't understand how anybody can possibly prefer a pale white or grey house to one with a passionate, joyful color. How can they call the God-given painted colors of grapes, of oranges, of pink seashells ugly colors? Why are they so disturbed by them, calling them Koolaid purple, soda pop orange, bubble gum pink, not to mention swimming pool blue and some of the others? He just can't understand.

Nata and Marta listen to Paco as he goes on and on, with his hands moving this way, then that way. As he talks and gestures, the two women move their eyes around the room. There are orange chairs and orange pillows, orange lamps and orange pictures. They smile when Paco mentions that orange, actually the color of Orange Crush, was Frank Sinatra's favorite color. He, himself, likes orange because he grew up surrounded by orange trees, and isn't the smell of fresh orange blossoms the smell of heaven?

After finishing their glasses of fresh orange juice, all three of them go visit the lime green house next door, where they meet Cynthia, and then Nata, Marta, Paco, and Cynthia go off together to see the owner of the bright canary yellow house, the house that turns out to belong to Felipe, who turns out to own eighty-five yellow singing canaries.

All of them then wind up at Nata's pink seashell house, where they spend the rest of the night talking about their plan of attack, over shots of tequila and under the careful watch of Emiliano Zapata's poster.

The next day they all receive a call from the mayor's office, saying that the city is receiving too many complaints, that the colors of their houses are way too loud, that they are hurting property values, people's eyes, and that, accordingly, he has no recourse but to require them to repaint their houses. The message is that his office is asking nicely, that he knows they will comply with the wishes of the community, since property values, as they know, are the bottom line.

Well, that day the group again gathers at Nata's house to prepare for battle. They first call themselves the

"De Colores Group." They pick the song "De Colores" to be their war song, and the flag with the brilliant colors of the rainbow — red, orange, yellow, green, blue, indigo, and violet — as their war flag. Their war cry becomes "Houses of Color for People of Color."

The next morning, with their flag waving high, they march through the streets of the city over to the mayor's office. As they march, they chant, "Houses of Color for People of Color," and they break out in song with "De Colores," about the brilliant colors of spring, of birds, of rainbows, and of the greatest loves.

The mayor quickly runs out of his big office upon hearing that the unruly mob from the shocking houses is making its way over to see him. When the De Colores Group stands toe to toe with the mayor and the sheriff and the deputies out in the middle of the street in front of City Hall, Nata raises the flag and the group instantly explodes out in song. As the war song rings through the air, the mayor and the sheriff and the deputies just stand there, looking from this way to that, shifting from this foot to that. When the song is about over, Nata slips the mayor a scroll. The mayor very carefully unrolls the lime green paper scroll as though it contains a red stick of lit dynamite. After he finishes reading the note, he smiles awkwardly at the group and says that he really enjoyed the song, that he actually was tempted to join in with them, since that is one of his very favorite, no, his very favorite song, in all the world.

Nata then steps forward, and squarely confronting the mayor, tells him not to change the tune, that just because he now knows that they know he is up for reelection, he shouldn't try seducing them, what with his slimy politician ways, into boring white houses.

The mayor insists that he would not dare insult them in such a way, that all he's asking is that they join him in his office for a fresh pot of hot coffee and a box of fresh doughnuts, of all kinds.

Nata retorts that she always knew that all their hard-earned tax money went into buying doughnuts, of all kinds, for the mayor, and that he looks like he should eat fewer doughnuts, and use the money saved to give City Hall a much-needed splash of color—perhaps cobalt blue—to go with his blue eye contacts, and that their colorful houses would not sting the mayor's eyes if only he looked with his natural dark brown eyes.

The mayor laughs nervously, showing two gold teeth, and begs them to please come inside for just a moment. The group hesitates, but then slowly filters into his office, which contains a big round table.

They reluctantly take seats around the table, and then the mayor starts. He starts with the calls, the letters, the meetings he is getting bombarded with, the studies that show that property values are hurt with such bright houses, the complaints of headaches, sore eyes caused by just looking at them. Look, he continues, it has nothing to do with the fact that they're Mexican. Look, he is Mexican himself. It is just that such bright colors, well . . .

Then the mayor suddenly gets silent. But everyone there knows what thoughts are now rattling about in his big, sweaty, watermelon head, what words he is swallowing, suppressing: That such garish colors announce, no, *shout* that Mexicans, and poor Mexicans, not Americanized Mexicans, live there—Mexicans who play loud *ranchero* music, who speak Spanish, who watch Mexican *telenovelas* on the Spanish TV channel. Yes, Mexicans who cook with smelly spices—garlic, onion, cumin—who crack piñatas in their backyards for all their hundreds of fiestas each year, who have eight, nine, even ten children, all playing on the street outside, all running around all the time in street gangs. Yes, Mexicans with the purple houses, the red houses, the green houses, who string Christmas lights on their roofs, their windows, one Christmas, and then never, ever take them down again.

Nata is silent, and then quietly asks the mayor whether his eyes hurt seeing red apples, orange kittens, yellow sunflowers, green trees, the blue ocean, purple grapes, violet sunsets, or the magical colors of a rainbow after a strong, cleansing rain. Nata reminds the mayor that the pyramids in Mexico were once painted in bright colors, that his red-and-yellow power tie is quite passionate, and that they know exactly what he's thinking, but doesn't dare say.

The mayor, visibly sweating, says that he doesn't want any trouble, that he hears them, but they also need to understand that the majority of the city thinks their bright houses are making the city look like a Fred Flintstone cartoon, that, as mayor, he has to see all sides, represent all sides, and come up with a solution, a compromise. He then stands up and announces that he is willing to pay, and pay out of his very own pocket, and not out of the city's doughnut fund, as they like to refer to it, for however many pails of paint it takes to repaint each of their houses. And, that he is even willing to go further than that: He will even pay to have their houses actually repainted for them.

And then he continues that all they have to do is agree to choose some nice colors. Now, they don't have to pick white or grey or beige. Light blues or pinks, pastels are just fine. And, by the way, there's just one more little thing: And that is that he's required to inform them, to put them on notice that, actually, their houses have been found in violation of a little code, a little law, but that, of course, now there's no problem, since he's getting their houses repainted for them, and for free.

At this, Nata jumps up from her seat, and taking hold of the flag, storms out with the group, leaving the mayor stunned, standing by his full box of doughnuts of all kinds.

Nata and the group then gather again at her pink seashell house to plan their next battle move. They wonder whether they should sue, whether they should buy several cans of red and green paint for Halloween and go paint great big polka dots on all the houses, including City Hall. They then wonder whether they should retaliate by painting their houses black. But they quickly abandon this idea, understanding, now, that the war is not at all about bright colors.

A week later, the local city paper runs a story about an amazing house, with each wall, each side, a different color: grape purple, orange orange, seashell pink, and canary yellow. The roof tile is lime green, the front door watermelon red. The caption under the bright color picture of the house reads that the house was just bought and repainted by a rich, celebrated artist, "Smith." Then in a flash, the war of color passes, without a drop of red blood, a purple war cry, or even a white whisper—nothing except the very loud, very colorful "Emiliano Zapata" party, with twenty mariachis and five fantastic piñatas, that "Smith" threw for the "De Colores Group," to which the mayor was not invited.

The Polka Dot Dress

I storm in. The metal green screen door bangs shut. My mother turns, knowing something's up. With beads of sweat on my forehead and shortness of breath, I announce that my mother must immediately teach me to dance the Spanish dance.

My mother, perplexed, grabs hold of me and tells me to calm down. I gulp for air. It's clear that I ran all the way home from school.

"What Spanish dance?" my mother asks.

"The Spanish dance in which you wear a red dress with black polka dots."

My mother finds the request quite strange since I have never shown the slightest interest in dance, or dresses, for that matter.

"Why do you want to learn that Spanish dance?"

I grin sheepishly. I then announce that my teacher, Mrs. Oliver, picked me to be in the school show, and that I'm to dance a Spanish dance in a polka dot dress.

"When's the show?"

"Next Friday, in the school auditorium."

"Is your whole class dancing this Spanish dance?"

"No, just me. I'm doing it solo."

My mother is stunned. "Well, let's at least see this polka dot dress you keep talking about."

"What polka dot dress? I have to get one. Can you make me one?"

"Hold on, now. You mean that next Friday, which is a week from now, you are going to perform a Spanish dance, solo, before the entire school auditorium, and you don't know the first thing about dancing, much less Spanish dancing, and you don't have the polka dot dress you're to dance in? How is it that the teacher picked you for this?"

"I volunteered."

"You volunteered? You're telling me that you volunteered to do something you know absolutely nothing about? This really doesn't make any sense whatsoever!"

I look down, and then say that I didn't get a part in the Christmas play, that they were all making fun of me, saying that I was so fat and had such a big nose that I wouldn't even make a good donkey for the mangy manger. When the teacher said that she needed someone to dance a Spanish dance before the play began and asked whether anyone had any experience, my arm had unexpectedly shot straight up.

My mother stares at me in disbelief, shaking her head. "Go talk to Nora, ask her if she can help you out. I don't know the first thing about Spanish dances, especially one you dance wearing a polka dot dress."

I walk dejectedly over to Nora's house. I feel so stupid. Why did I ever volunteer? I should just go over and tell the teacher I lied about everything, that I don't know the first thing about anything, much less dancing. But I'm so tired of never getting picked for anything, of feeling so different. Well, now, thanks to my stupidity, everyone will know what a misfit I really am, that they were right all along not to want to have anything to do with me.

I ring the doorbell. Nora comes to the door and is surprised to see me. She can never think of a time when I have come by to visit alone, without my mother. Nora invites me in and pours me a glass of orange pop. She then asks how school is going. I stammer, and then blurt out that I need Nora to teach me to dance in Spanish. Nora laughs and slaps her knees when I explain that I want to learn the Spanish dance in which you wear a red dress with black polka dots and that, no, I don't have the polka dot dress, and that the show is this coming Friday, and that, by the way, I'm to dance solo, which I unexpectedly volunteered for.

After Nora finally stops laughing, she asks me to help her move the furniture in the living room to make some space. Nora then looks through a pile of dusty records, picks one, and starts the record player. Her feet go this way, then that way, her hands are here, then there, her body and head sway and turn. Now I'm more convinced than ever before about what a complete idiot I am to have volunteered. I never realized how complicated and difficult dancing flamenco, as Nora called the Spanish dance, could be. I continued to watch in bewilderment as Nora continues to move to the music in sharp and precise movements.

After dancing for a while, Nora takes my hands and pulls me to my feet. She tells me to follow her moves, that I must learn to feel, to really feel the music. I feel awkward, stiff, and stupid. I try, but it's impossible. Nora then stops dancing and starts coaching me, adjusting the movements of my arms, legs, body, and head. After about an hour of what seems more like octopus dancing than any type of flamenco dancing, Nora turns the record player off and instructs me to come back tomorrow.

When I return home, I find my mother on the phone, laughing hysterically. I know exactly whom she's talking to. I want to die. I can't believe what I've gotten myself into. Everyone will die laughing at me. It now seems surprisingly preferable to have remained invisible.

"Nora tells me you're a regular Carmen Miranda."

I've heard of this Carmen Miranda. She's the one who dances with a ridiculous mountain of fruit on her head. I don't say anything. I let myself fall heavily onto the sofa.

"Come now. Nora says you are coming along nicely. Just a bit more practice, that's all."

I remain silent, grim. My mother then walks over to me and tells me to go see her friend Lydia tomorrow, that perhaps she can help out with that polka dot dress I need.

The next day I get the same reaction from Lydia as I did from Nora. Lydia, after laughing forever, proclaims that there is absolutely no way in the world she can measure, cut, sew, and finish a dress in time for the show, especially that type of polka dot dress. All she can suggest is that I try to rent one.

After school the next day, my mother and I go over to a place that rents costumes for parties and Halloween. After walking around among the hairy gorilla suits and frilly ballerina tutus, I wander off to the women's section. There, between fuzz, feathers, and furs, I find it: It's red with big black polka dots, with puffy sleeves and a white multi-layered bottom. The only problem is that it's a woman's size fourteen. I convince my mother to rent it, anyway.

I practice my steps religiously every day after school at Nora's. And every day after that, I come home and perform for my mother on top of the kitchen table. Every single muscle in my body is now sore to the bone.

When Friday finally comes, I put on the polka dot dress, and my mother spends a full hour stapling the dress with hundreds of metal staples to make it fit. She then combs my long hair back in a bun, places a big red hibiscus flower behind my ear, and paints my lips bright red with lipstick.

We drive to school, with me standing in the back, afraid to pop open any of the hundreds of staples. After the initial welcome remarks by the principal, I walk onto the stage in my brilliant red polka dot dress. The music starts. I start. I turn and move with the music, gracefully, but precisely, like a flamenco dancer. My new black patent leather shoes sound smartly on the wooden floor. Then the audience applauds, loudly. I beam, feeling magical, even a bit special, for once.

When I later watch the Christmas play, I smile, thinking their parts seem so simple.

The Wooden Saints

Tomás sits on a turned-over pail, watching the strange saint emerge from the curls of wood: Saint Jerome, the saint of learning. This is the saint Tomás requested from Jorge, the *santero*. Instead of a book, however, this Saint Jerome has a carved bottle of beer in his right hand. Tomás wonders whether he'll now become an alcoholic with the help of this saint, rather than get the supposed help he desperately needs with school. While Jorge works the wood with his hands, he asks the boy about school, how he's doing. Tomás just shrugs his shoulders and then says that it is his mother who wants him to get the saint.

Tomás had begged to go to the other *santero*. But, according to his mother, that *santero* is for the tourists, who know nothing about saints, and Jorge is the real *santero* with the saints that work. Tomás does not understand. The other *santero* carves saints to look like saints, like the drawings of saints he has seen in a book and at the church.

Tomás looks at one of Jorge's saints that is sitting on the porch to dry. It is about a foot and a half tall. It has purple hair, red ears, a green beard, and one hand holds a blue guitar, the other a red piñata in the shape of a strawberry. One foot wears a sandal; the other is a peg leg. When Tomás finally manages to get Jorge's attention, he points to the saint on the porch and asks just who that might be. Jorge turns to look and states that, of course, that is Saint Barbara, as though it is quite obvious.

Tomás is about to ask how exactly Saint Barbara got her peg leg, when he notices Jorge starting to carve a cigar into his Saint Jerome. Tomás gets to his feet and leaves, angry about how his saint is turning out.

When he gets home, he runs into his mother, who is feeding their little pregnant dog. She asks about his Saint Jerome. Tomás doesn't respond. He just goes to his room and falls into his bed. He hates his Saint Jerome. He hates Jorge and his embarrassing saints. He hates his section of town for being so stupid, so backwards to believe in wooden saints.

The saint stuff is just a bunch of nonsense, just more dumb Mexican stuff and superstition. Even if saints were real people once, they're dead now. It's absurd to think that a dumb piece of wood is a saint, who is going to help you just because you pray to it, or build it some gaudy altar in your home, or give it food offerings of tacos and beer. No such nonsense is ever seen on TV in those nice houses.

After a while, Tomás gets out of bed, takes the money his mother gave him for the saint from Jorge, and leaves the house. He walks about a mile and enters a store. There he finds the other *santero* sitting behind a desk and a stack of paper. Tomás asks for a Saint Jerome. The *santero* says he has five in stock. He then walks to the back of the store, returning with one of the five identical-looking Saint Jeromes. Tomás takes the regular-looking saint and pays the *santero*. He then walks home with the saint in a brown paper bag, and once there, he puts the saint on his desk.

Tomás's mother asks him the next day about the saint she found on his desk. She asks him where he got it. Tomás replies that he got him from the *santero*. The mother then says that she has now done all she can to help him with school, that she gave him the little she had saved to get him a Saint Jerome that worked, not that tourist saint he got from that other *santero*. He can't fool her. If he flunks out, if he has to repeat a grade, or if they put him in a school for the retarded because he can't understand English, he has no one to blame but himself, for being so obstinate, so full of unrealistic ideas from all the TV he watches.

Tomás is silent. But then he yells back: He says that if she had not been a farmworker, if she had had an education, if she knew English, he would not be in the mess he's in. It is her fault, not his. She is crazy to think that buying him a saint made out of wood is actually going to do something to help him. This only helps to do one thing: to get even more people at school to make fun of him. Why couldn't he just have had a regular mother, like those on TV. Why does she have to be so different, so strange, just like Jorge's strange and absurd wooden saints?

While Tomás is at school the next day, the mother goes and answers the front door. It is Jorge, the *santero*. The mother opens the door and lets him in. Jorge hands the mother the finished Saint Jerome. Besides the beer bottle and cigar, Jorge's Saint Jerome has a long green feather sticking out of his head and a pair of bright orange roller skates on his feet.

The mother smiles and comments on how nice the saint turned out. But then she escorts him to Tomás's desk and shows him the other Saint Jerome. The mother says her son is a burro, who has gotten too big for his pants by watching too much TV. Please don't feel insulted by the boy's rude behavior. Jorge nods quietly and leaves, taking his Saint Jerome back with him.

A week later Tomás mentions to his mother in passing that he will start staying an hour after school each day, that his teacher is showing some interest in him and wants to help him with his English. He also says that one of the white boys in class invited him over to his house on Saturday to look over some of his new comic books.

Then one day Tomás returns home carrying Jorge's

Saint Jerome in front of him with both of his hands. He walks to his desk and replaces the other Saint Jerome with Jorge's.

Tomás tells his mother that Jorge, the *santero*, had come to see him today after school. He told him about a little girl who had come crying to his house that morning about her dog. She wanted a saint for her dog, a saint that would bring him back to life, a saint that would take away that car that killed him and left him flat in the middle of the road in front of her house. Jorge had then asked Tomás whether he could buy one of the five puppies just born to his dog. Tomás tells his mother that he gave Jorge the best puppy to take to the little girl, and that he now understands why Jorge's wooden saints are the ones that work.

The Flamingos

The young girl is helping her grandmother wrap the gift. Her job is to hold the wrapping paper while her grandmother cuts a piece of scotch tape and tapes the paper down. They are using the Sunday funny papers for wrapping paper. It was the girl's idea. Her grandmother was going to use a square of thin white paper she found in an old shoe box, but the girl convinced her otherwise, pointing at the dogs, cats, and funny people in the funny papers, all colorful and lively. She said that the funny papers were better to wrap the gift with since Lala, her grandmother's sister, could then enjoy looking at the funny characters after opening her gift. They would make her laugh.

Her grandmother says she can still use the white paper for a bow. She then folds and refolds the white piece of paper, transforming it into a beautiful white bird.

The girl suggests painting the bird pink to match the gift they are giving Lala. Her grandmother agrees, and so the girl takes a bottle of pink nail polish and starts turning the white bird pink. Her grandmother gets up and opens all the windows since the smell of the nail polish makes them cough.

When finished, the girl places the pink bird on top of a jar lid and then puts it on the window by her bed to dry. It takes an entire hour for the bird to dry, and it probably would have taken much longer had the girl not blown on it the entire time.

The girl then takes the bird to her grandmother. Her grandmother is quite pleased with the little pink bird, but asks whether it doesn't need a couple of eyes to see. The girl takes a black crayon and puts two dots for eyes on one side of the bird's head. The grandmother notes that now no one will think the bird has only one eye. She then tapes the bird to the box they just finished wrapping. The bird stands and looks as though it is about to take off in flight. Now finished, the young girl and her grandmother stand and clap their hands, happy with their creation, their gift for Lala.

They had wanted to buy a nice package of pretty blue wrapping paper sprinkled with silver stars and a bright yellow bow at the store. But there had been no money left, after getting Lala what she told them she wanted for her seventieth birthday, what would make her really happy.

A week ago, Lala came to visit them, just as she did every day. But this time, she came with a fat rolled-up newspaper under her right arm. The girl had been coloring an egg shell with her crayons. Her grandmother had been braiding her long white hair.

"Look here," Lala announced, as she marched into their room and unrolled the newspaper like a pirate's map. "This is what I want for my birthday." She pointed to a drawing of two flamingos that were being advertised at Winn's for $7.95.

"Oh, they are nice," the girl's grandmother said, "What color do you want?"

"Pink. They only come in pink. I mean, have you ever seen or heard of a green or a blue flamingo?" Lala said, rolling her eyes.

The grandmother just shrugged her shoulders. Lala visited for ten more minutes, then left because she had to water her lawn. She added that a pair of pink flamingos would sure look nice on her green grass.

Once Lala left, the girl turned to her grandmother and asked, "Do you really think she can keep flamingos on her grass? Won't they fly away?"

"No, no," her grandmother laughed. "The flamingos she wants are not real; they are made of plastic."

"Well, we don't have money to buy her even plastic flamingos, do we? Maybe we can make her some."

"I'm afraid we can't make the type of flamingos she wants. I wish we could, though, since we don't have $7.95."

"But she really seems to want them."

"Well, I think I have $4.50. Let's go and buy her at least one flamingo."

The next day they woke up early, dressed quickly, and drank two cups of coffee each. They then walked two miles downtown, to the other side of town, and finally stumbled upon Winn's, after noticing the advertisement for the flamingos scotch-taped to one of the store's glass windows. They went inside. The store had wide aisles, shiny floors, and bright lights. Things made of wire, metal, plastic, and glass were in steel bins and in rows and stacks and piles everywhere. After twenty minutes of feeling like they were walking around in circles, the girl shyly approached a saleslady wearing big brown loafers and pointed to the flamingo advertisement on the window. The saleslady said something in English, but when she realized that neither the girl nor the old woman understood, she pointed to the left rear corner of the store.

When they got to the very end of the store, they saw two pink plastic flamingos standing on top of a big pile of white boxes. They carefully examined each of the boxes and found that they all contained pairs of flamingos.

"Why don't we open a box and take out just one flamingo," the girl suggested. Her grandmother agreed, telling her not to forget the legs. So the girl got a box, opened it carefully, and pulled out one of the pink flamingos inside, as well as a pair of legs. She then closed the box and put the box back in the pile.

The girl, with the plastic pink flamingo wrapped in her arms, and her grandmother, with the pair of long flamingo legs in hers, walked to the checkout counter. The grandmother gave the girl $4.50, which the girl handed to the cashier. The cashier said something in English they couldn't understand. They looked at each other, then at the cashier. The cashier spoke again in English and then made the peace sign. The girl told her grandmother that the cashier would not let them buy just one flamingo, that they could only buy a box of two.

They left the flamingo with the cashier and took back the $4.50. Feeling quite disappointed, they kicked small rocks with their sneakers all the way home.

When they finally got home, all dusty and thirsty, the girl went out and picked twelve big yellow lemons from the lemon tree outside. Her grandmother made them a big pitcher of lemonade, so sour it made them pucker like prunes with every sip. Drinking lemonade made them feel better, and so they began to plan how to get the three dollars and forty-five cents they still needed to get Lala the pink flamingos she had her heart set on.

As they were about to finish the whole pitcher of lemonade, Lala walked in. She took a chair and planted herself directly in front of the girl's grandmother. She then started to talk about nothing, her two big eyes moving up and down and all around the room, looking for the box of flamingos she thought they got her. She heard that earlier the girl and her grandmother had gone to town. When she could not spot them in their room, she left, saying she wanted to say something to the girl's mother. Lala then proceeded from room to room, looking everywhere for the box of pink flamingos, and finally left in a huff.

"She was looking all over for the flamingos she thinks we bought her," the girl said.

"I know," her grandmother responded, pushing her lips together and making them look like a single line. "Go get my walking stick. We have work to do." The girl brought her the walking stick, which was really just a tree branch that the girl smoothed out, painted blue, and gave to her one Christmas.

"Are we going up the hill?" the girl asked.

"Yes. We will take my straw basket and gather some medicine plants."

"What are the plants for? Is someone sick?"

"No. No. We will sell them to Inés at the *mercado*."

Inés was a loud woman with big red hair, who ran a small shop at the *mercado*. The shop had shelves and shelves of brightly painted clay saints and angels. The faces of the saints frightened the girl: Their faces were chalk white with big open glass eyes and long eyelashes. The saints had special powers, with each saint specializing in a certain magic, or so the girl heard. Inés's shop always had three tall white candles burning, which made it smell like the inside of a church, sweet and smoky. On a spinning wheel of wire hung square packages with plants inside. These were the medicine plants.

With walking stick and basket in hand, the girl and her grandmother started their journey up the hill, about a quarter mile from the house. As they slowly climbed higher and higher, the grandmother searched about for certain plants, while making a peculiar soft humming sound. She had instructed the girl to be quiet and to study what she did with the medicine plants, since she wanted the girl to learn how to use their special healing powers.

When they finally reached the top of the hill, the grandmother walked to the east side and pointed to a cluster of small plants. She bent down and carefully selected and picked a handful of them. She tied the little bunch of plants together with a piece of string she took from her pocket. This particular plant, she told the girl, heals the heart. They walked to the south side of the hill. There she picked another handful of plants, and after tying them together, placed them in the basket. Next, they proceeded to the west side and then to the north side of the hill. At each spot, she picked a handful of a different plant, tied it into a bundle, and put it in her basket, carefully explaining to the girl the special traits and magic of each particular plant. After they had walked all around the hill in a circle, they started all over again. They went east, south, west, and then north. These are the four directions, the grandmother told the girl, the directions of the four winds, of the four windows in our lives. After they had filled the basket, they started down the hill. Halfway down, they sat on the grass and gazed at the maroon and orange of the evening sky. They then continued home.

"Tomorrow we will go and sell these medicine plants to Inés," the grandmother said to the girl.

"Why don't you sell her plants more often? We could become rich, you and me. We could pick plants for her every day."

"I only sell medicine plants to Inés in an emergency and only if I can label them myself. Inés doesn't understand the first thing about plants and about using them to help heal people. All she cares about is making money. The last time I visited her shop, I took a look at the packages of medicine plants she had hanging on her spinning wheel of wire. They were labeled all wrong. The packages had titles like: chicken pox tea, weight loss tea, pimple tea. The worst one said that it was good for headaches, hemorrhoids, sore throats, indigestion, vaginal infections, and weight loss. I know you don't understand all this. All I'm saying is that Inés mislabels her plants to sell them quickly to people who know even less about plants, but trust her to know.

"When I was there last, Inés asked me to bring her some new medicine plants. I said I would, but only if she would let me label them myself. She agreed, so tomorrow we'll take the basket of medicine plants we picked today. You can help me package and label them there."

"How much will she give us for all the magic plants?"

"About three dollars."

"But we need more than that for the flamingos."

"I know. I'll make some paper flowers tomorrow out of crepe paper, and you can help me sell them at the *mercado*. We won't leave the *mercado* until we make forty-five cents. All right?"

"All right," the girl responded, feeling somewhat anxious about how she'd do selling flowers, since she'd never had to sell anything before.

The next morning the grandmother woke the girl up at six. They quickly washed and drank two strong cups of coffee each. The grandmother then reached under her bed and pulled out a long green cardboard box, out of which she took a sheet of bright pink crepe paper. She then brought out a pair of scissors and a spool of thin wire.

The girl watched as her grandmother molded, cut, and wired the pretty pink crepe paper into a beautiful flower. She then gave the flower a stem and leaves, using green crepe paper and wire. Her grandmother performed like a magician, producing flower after flower. Each time she finished one, she gave it to the girl to hold. At the end, the girl held thirteen big, bright paper flowers in her hands: two pink ones, two yellow, four blue, and five red ones. Her grandmother noted that she made more red ones because most everyone else preferred their flowers red rather than blue, which was their favorite color. She then took one of the pretty blue flowers and gave it to the girl to keep, telling her that it was the best one of all.

They walked to the *mercado*, which was four blocks away on their side of town. The grandmother carried the basket with the medicine plants, while the girl carried the colorful bouquet of paper flowers.

After reaching the *mercado*, the grandmother led the girl through the intertwining and narrow corridors, where colorful piñatas made out of papier-mâché and shaped like donkeys and strawberries and other festive forms hung from shop roofs like Christmas ornaments. There were wooden shelves with rows and rows of Mexican candy: sweet pumpkin candy pieces, white coconut squares, wooden tins filled with soft caramel, which had to be eaten with a small wooden spoon. There were wooden carts with round glass jars as tall as the girl, filled with bright red watermelon water, white *horchata* milk, reddish tamarind water, and freshly made orange juice. Big chunks of white ice floated like icebergs inside the huge glass jars. A big woman with long, black braided hair and wearing a loose yellow dress with embroidered flowers pushed a cart with wheels in front of her shouting "hot tamales." A small Indian-looking man stood at a corner, selling hot ears of yellow corn, which he flavored with white mayonnaise and red chili pepper.

With the girl in tow, the grandmother quickly navigated the maze of the *mercado* and found Inés at her shop, peeling a ripe yellow mango. The girl's grandmother and Inés greeted each other with a warm hug and kiss, and then turned and smiled at the girl, who quietly stood back, holding the paper flowers.

"Come here," the grandmother said, motioning to the girl.

When the girl approached them, Inés gave her a warm hug, telling her how much she'd grown and admired the colorful paper flowers in her hands. Inés then turned to the girl's grandmother and thanked her for finally bringing her some real medicine plants.

She also added that, as promised, she would let her package and label them.

The girl followed her grandmother to the back of Inés's small shop and assisted her as she carefully placed each little bunch of plants into a small plastic bag. Her grandmother then labeled each package with a note explaining the healing and medicinal power of the special plant inside.

After hanging and arranging the packages of medicine plants on Inés's spinning wheel of wire, they were done. The grandmother then found Inés busy calling customers on the phone, telling them to come quickly since she had just received a new batch of powerful medicine plants from the best and wisest plant witch around. In between calls, Inés thanked and hugged them both goodbye, and then handed an envelope to the girl's grandmother.

"What did Inés give you?" asked the girl.

The girl's grandmother reached into her pocket and pulled out the envelope. She opened it slowly and found three dollars inside. "Well, now, with these three dollars, we only need to sell enough flowers to make forty-five cents more," she told the girl. "And if we sell more, we'll buy a great big tall glass of that cold watermelon water I saw you eyeing. We'll get two of those red-and-white striped straws and make funny noises blowing bubbles with them." The girl broke into a bright smile at the thought.

After dividing the colorful paper flowers, the grandmother handed half to the girl and asked her to stand at the entrance to the *mercado*. She was to ask for a nickel for one flower, a dime for three. She added that she would try selling her flowers by walking up and down the various walkways in the *mercado,* and that she would come see the girl in an hour.

The girl first walked over to where her grandmother asked her to stand. She then watched as her grandmother slowly walked away. She counted her flowers: three red, one blue, one yellow, one pink. She recounted them: One pink, one yellow, one blue, three red. She then took a quick look around, noticing all the people moving up and down like big ants. Suddenly, she felt like running after her grandmother and telling her she didn't want to be alone, didn't know the first thing about selling flowers, or selling anything for that matter, that no one would want to buy anything from her. But then she stopped and thought about how much Lala wanted those pink flamingos and how much her grandmother, especially, wanted Lala to have them. So she continued to stand there, flowers in hand, eyes on flowers, or sometimes on the floor, while people passed by.

Twenty minutes passed, and the girl had not sold one flower. She felt quite bad. She wondered how many her grandmother had sold. Then she noticed a pair of black cowboy boots in front of her.

"Nice flowers. Did you make them?" she heard the boots say.

"My grandmother made them. I helped her. We want to sell them to buy pink flamingos," the girl forced herself to say. She then looked up and noticed that the boots were attached to a tall man in a cowboy hat and dark suit.

"Pink flamingos, huh? How much for one flower?" the man asked.

"A nickel, three for a dime."

"How about if I give you a dollar for all your pretty flowers? That way you can buy a whole lot of pink flamingos."

The girl beamed. The man gave her a crisp new dollar bill; she gave him all her paper flowers. When the man in boots left, the girl examined the dollar bill, placed it in her pocket, and let out a little squeal of joy. She couldn't believe she had sold her flowers. She just couldn't believe it. She thought she would not even sell one flower. But she had sold all of them, and for a whole lot more than she ever thought possible. She couldn't wait to tell her grandmother.

The girl waited for her grandmother, picturing how happy she would be to hear about the man in the boots and the dollar. She also amused herself looking at all the piñatas hanging about her, wondering which one she wished for her birthday. She waved when she finally spotted her grandmother coming towards her.

"What happened to all your flowers?" the grandmother asked. The girl proceeded to tell her about the man in the boots and then pulled out the dollar bill. The grandmother hugged her, telling her what a good business woman she was. As for her, she had only been able to sell two of the flowers, the two red ones. They went and celebrated with a glass of watermelon water and two red-and-white straws.

Upon returning home from the *mercado,* they placed the remaining paper flowers in the same bottle with the girl's blue one. Then in came Lala. She looked them up and down, and then proceeded to survey the room like a rotating radar. The girl and her grandmother knew exactly what she was looking for. When it became evident to Lala that there was no box of flamingos in the room, she left and searched the rest of the house. She then returned with a pout on her face. She asked about "those paper flowers" in the bottle, and then stated that she hoped no one would even think of giving her paper flowers for her birthday since she had plenty of them already. She then turned and left in a huff, just as before.

The next day, Lala's birthday, the girl and her grandmother woke up early and again walked over to Winn's. They bought a set of flamingos just in time since there were only two boxes left.

Later they walked over to Lala's house, proudly carrying their gift wrapped in funny paper with the pink paper bird for a bow. The house was full of moving, talking, laughing people, mostly relatives. Many came and warmly greeted the girl's grandmother, and then patted the girl's head, saying how much she'd grown. The girl followed her grandmother as she weaved through the crowded house. They finally came upon Lala.

Lala sat like a Buddha on a big cushioned pink chair in the living room. She wore a pink dress, and a pair of pink flamingo earrings hung from her ears. When she saw the girl's grandmother and the girl, she motioned towards a long table next to her, which was piled with gifts. They placed their gift there, and then joined the room in standing and singing the "Happy Birthday" song. In came a large, round shocking pink cake lit up like a fireball with seventy candles. People made room for the traveling cake, afraid their hair might catch on fire.

The cake was presented to Lala. She closed her eyes, made a wish, and then spent the next five minutes trying to blow out all the candles. The crowd applauded. Pieces of pink cake on pink paper plates and Mexican chocolate in pink paper cups were then distributed and enjoyed by all. While the girl sipped her hot chocolate, she turned and whispered to her grandmother that she thought they would make Lala's birthday wish come true. Her grandmother smiled, agreeing. The girl couldn't eat a single bite of her cake because she couldn't wait to see Lala's expression when she opened their gift and found the pink flamingos.

It finally came time for the gifts. Everyone crowded around Lala and her table of gifts. Commenting on the colorful wrapping paper, Lala picked out the one with the pink paper bird for a bow. She looked for a card saying who it was from. Suddenly, the girl jumped up and exclaimed that it was from her and her grandmother. Lala smiled, and then proceeded to unwrap and open the box. She happily pulled out the pair of pink plastic flamingos, saying how beautiful they were, exactly what she had wished for. She then held them up in the air for everyone to see. The girl was so happy to have given Lala what she wanted, to have made her so happy, to have made her birthday wish come true.

But the girl checked herself when she noticed the awkward expression on other people's faces. She finally understood why. Lala opened the next box and found another pair of plastic pink flamingos. The third was the same as the fourth. At the end, Lala found herself surrounded by twenty plastic pink flamingos. She looked quite disappointed.

"What will you do with all these flamingos?" someone finally asked. Lala thought for awhile, then she said she would put them in the front yard. She got off her pink chair and took the flamingos and guests outside, where they helped her arrange all twenty flamingos on the grass.

The only one at the party who did not follow Lala outside with her flamingos was the girl. She told her grandmother that she was not feeling well and was going home. When the grandmother returned from the party, she found the girl in bed. When she asked how she was feeling, the girl didn't respond. She just turned her face to the wall and then finally fell asleep.

The next morning the girl told her grandmother that they might as well have given Lala paper flowers for her birthday since the pink flamingos they worked so hard to get her weren't special at all, not with the millions of stupid flamingos she wound up getting.

"Our gift will be the best," the grandmother responded, "because our special gift to Lala has just begun."

"What do you mean?"

"Just wait until dark. You'll understand."

When night finally came, the girl followed her grandmother to Lala's front yard. There she found the twenty flamingos arranged in a "V" like flying geese. Her grandmother whispered her plan to the girl, and then they set to work, moving the flamingos around, one by one, and forming them into a great big circle, like elephants following each other in a circus. They giggled in the dark, and once done, they snuck back home and went to bed.

The next morning, they suddenly woke up to the sound of pounding on their window. It was an excited Lala. They let her in.

"The flamingos, they moved! They're all in a circle now!" Lala exclaimed, shaking all over.

"What are you talking about? Calm down now. How about a cup of tea?" the grandmother said, as she started to comb her long white hair slowly. The girl worked to hide a smile.

"No, you two are coming with me," Lala declared, as she dragged them both outside to her front yard. The girl took her cues from her grandmother and feigned disbelief and amazement in finding the flamingos walking around in a circle. Her grandmother convinced Lala not to worry, and that, in fact, the flamingos looked better in a circle, rather than in that "V" shape they were in before, which made them look like flying geese, anyway.

That night the grandmother and girl returned to the flamingos, but this time they arranged them in pairs so that they appeared to be kissing each other.

As expected, Lala showed up early at their door the next morning. This time she walked around in circles, convinced that the twenty flamingos were haunted, that they'd moved around again and that this time they'd formed themselves into kissing pairs. She then dragged them both out again and showed them the haunted flamingos.

After pretending to be alarmed by the moving flamingos, the girl observed her grandmother take out and light a cigarette. While puffing away, she told Lala that the flamingos did seem to be haunted. She then suggested that perhaps it was because Lala pressured everyone she knew to give her a set of flamingos for her birthday. Wishing for two flamingos, she wound up with twenty of them, which made everyone feel bad since their gift didn't seem so special anymore.

Lala fell silent. She then asked whether the girl's grandmother could cure the flamingos. The grandmother eventually agreed, but only if Lala agreed to help work the cure. She nodded hesitantly, and then asked what she would have to do exactly.

"First, bring me twenty blue glass bottles," the girl's grandmother told Lala, as she snuck a wink at the girl.

"Twenty blue bottles? What the hell for?" Lala snorted, waving her arms in the air like a big pelican.

"Look, you promised to help. If not, you're stuck with your herd of haunted flamingos. Who knows, you might wake up tomorrow morning and find them dancing around your bed."

"All right, but what's with the twenty blue bottles?"

"You have twenty flamingos, right?"

"Well, that explains everything. Silly of me to ask."

The grandmother and girl returned to their house. Once there, they fell into laughter, wondering where Lala would come up with twenty blue bottles.

While they listened to a story on the radio, Lala burst in, carrying four bottles. She was sweating and somewhat out of breath.

"I went everywhere, asked everyone, but was only able to find four blue bottles. Thank God some people around here are really bad cooks since all these bottles are bottles of milk of magnesia. And yes, because I know you'll ask, I did, indeed, thank everyone I saw for coming to my birthday party and for going to all that trouble getting me those pink flamingos I wanted. And no, I didn't say a word about them being haunted and all."

"Good. Now you'll just have to help us find sixteen empty soda bottles. We'll then all sit down and paint them blue with a certain can of paint I've saved up for emergencies just like this," stated the grandmother, as she smiled at the girl. She then asked the girl to go find as many empty pop bottles as she could, while Lala caught her breath. The girl left and returned about twenty minutes later with a cardboard box filled with all the bottles they needed.

After a quick cup of tea, they settled themselves outside on the porch and spent the rest of the afternoon painting the sixteen bottles blue. Once finished, the grandmother instructed Lala to show up at their house at nightfall and not to be late. This time Lala just agreed, not asking a single question.

Lala arrived at their door punctually at dusk. The grandmother explained the work ahead. They must take the twenty blue glass bottles to the flamingos, and then they must set one bottle under each one of them.

Accordingly, they gathered up the twenty bottles and stacked them carefully inside the cardboard box. They then carried the box to the flamingos. Once there, all three helped place one blue bottle under every pink flamingo. The grandmother explained, as they worked, that the spirits that were spooking the flamingos were of the mischievous type, and that such types were known to be particularly attracted to the color blue, which explained the blue bottles. The girl watched as Lala's eyes and round face bulged up like a bullfrog with questions she needed to ask, but all that came out of her was a long sigh. When they were done, the grandmother instructed Lala to show up at their house at sunrise with a new box of tissue. Lala nodded. They all returned home and went to sleep, although Lala stayed awake for hours wondering whether the blue bottles were working or how exactly they were supposed to work.

At sunrise, Lala was there with a big box of tissue. All three then marched off to the flamingos, with the grandmother heading up the little army. Once there, the grandmother gave them their marching orders: First, they must be quiet. The flamingos had not moved since the mischievous spirits had apparently taken the bait, the blue bottles, and they were inside the blue bottles now, one spirit in each bottle. Their job was to trap them inside the bottles by quietly, yet quickly stuffing the top of the bottles with a wad of tissue. Lala took her orders quite nervously.

They set off to do their serious work. They each took a stack of tissues and visually divided the bottles: The grandmother took ten, since she said she'd done this before, and the girl and Lala each took five. With tissues in hand and their plan of attack in mind, they charged forth.

At first, Lala hung back a bit and watched as the grandmother approached the first bottle. She quietly snuck up on it and quickly capped it shut with a ball of wadded-up tissue. She then moved on to the next bottle. Feeling somewhat more confident, Lala joined them in trapping the spirits in the bottles assigned to her.

Once everyone completed her assigned mission, they regrouped. The grandmother left them awhile and walked around and examined the twenty capped bottles. She returned with a grin, saying that the little spirits were all in there, trapped shut in the bottles. She then told Lala that the only thing left to do was to help them collect the bottles and take them to her room so that she could get rid of the twenty little devils once and for all.

Once the bottles were all gathered and deposited safely in the grandmother's room, Lala left, saying she was going to visit and admire her twenty little flamingos. The girl and her grandmother looked at their box of blue bottles and laughed out loud.

The next morning Lala came to visit, all excited. The flamingos did not move. The blue bottles apparently worked, and that was the best present ever. She was so happy. The grandmother smiled and so did the girl.

The Café

The first time the young boy ventures down into the dark basement by himself, he tears up screaming, something about a white ghost and its taking residence there. His ninety-year-old grandfather is able to calm him down by taking the boy to the basement and pulling off the white sheet the boy thought was the ghost. There is no ghost there, just an old dusty metal contraption, which the grandfather identifies as "Santo Pepe."

The boy examines the metal contraption carefully, moving some of its lids and knobs. He then turns to his grandfather and asks why the old machine, which looks like nothing more than an ancient coffee maker, is called Santo Pepe. The old man smiles and quietly explains that this is no ordinary coffee maker; it is Santo Pepe, a saint of sorts, who was once worshipped in the little stucco church of the town of Las Flores. When the boy asks why Santo Pepe is in the basement, the grandfather simply says that he won him in a bingo game.

It is a long, tangled story of sorts. Before Santo Pepe was in the basement, he stood between Saint Peter and Saint Paul in the white alcove at the altar of the church of Las Flores. There, the townspeople burned candles and prayed to it. But then all of this quickly changed when a stern old priest from the old world became the new priest of the church. Upon first catching sight of Santo Pepe, he cursed the pagan lot he had been assigned to, and then grabbed Santo Pepe, who at the time was wearing a brand new purple velvet robe of sorts, and dumped him unceremoniously in the garbage can outside. At mass that same day, the old priest scolded the townspeople, accusing them of being pagans, just like their Indian ancestors, for worshipping false gods like that metal contraption of a coffee maker he had discovered and tossed out that morning. As far as he was concerned, that contraption could not even brew a decent cup of coffee, much less perform the miracles he had been told about. If they did not want to wind up in hell, boiling in big vats of hot coffee, they better listen to him and stop being so backwards.

The townspeople quietly filtered out of the church with bowed heads. But once a safe distance from the stern and watchful eye of the old priest, they ran to the garbage can and retrieved Santo Pepe. That night in the town's plaza, after they knew the old priest had gone to bed, the mayor presided over a bingo game with the entire town in attendance. There, the boy's grandfather had yelled bingo and won the high privilege of taking Santo Pepe home. The grandfather built a little altar for Santo Pepe in his house, and for years the townspeople came there secretly to pay their respects with offerings of prayers, candles, and food. This continued until the grandfather lost his wife and left the little town.

The boy watches his grandfather boil water and then make himself a cup of coffee using a teaspoon of Sanka coffee. The boy then asks what sort of miracles the coffee maker, Santo Pepe, performed. His grandfather pokes a hole into a can of condensed milk with a small knife, pours a bit of milk into his coffee, and then stirs slowly, changing the color of the coffee from black to the warm color of caramel candy.

"It made coffee," the grandfather responds. The boy looks perplexed. He thinks to himself: A coffee maker makes coffee, that's what it's for, that's what it does, that's what it's supposed to do, so a coffee maker that makes coffee is no miracle. No wonder the old priest threw out their metal contraption.

"What kind of coffee?" the boy asks.

"Coffee, just coffee," the old man responds, sipping his coffee slowly. Sensing the boy's puzzlement, the grandfather asks the boy to go down to the basement and bring Santo Pepe.

After a few minutes, the boy returns carrying Santo Pepe in his arms. The boy then helps the old man give Santo Pepe a good cleaning in the kitchen sink with hot water, a box of soap, and a brush. Using two clean kitchen towels, they dry Santo Pepe to a nice shine.

The old man opens a door in the cupboard, takes down a white ceramic container, and pours a handful of dark whole coffee beans into a metal grinder. He then starts turning the little handle on the grinder, grinding the coffee beans into a coarse powder, as though he has done this many times before. He empties the ground coffee into a paper filter, pours fresh water into Santo Pepe, and then turns him on with a switch. All of a sudden, Santo Pepe starts rattling, smoking, and making hissing sounds. In a few minutes, thick black coffee like black oil starts pouring out of Santo Pepe into a glass pot. The old man takes the pot and pours the boy and himself a cup of the hot coffee. He hands one of the white ceramic cups to the boy and tells him to drink it slowly, quietly, and thoughtfully. He takes his cup, and they sit down at the wooden kitchen table by the open window. The boy mimics his grandfather and holds the cup carefully in both hands while he takes small sips, wondering the whole time what miracle he is about to experience.

After the boy finishes drinking the last drop of coffee in his cup, he taps his grandfather on the shoulder and shows him his empty cup. The old man nods, takes the boy's cup in both hands, and peers into the cup. The boy watches closely, wondering what his grandfather is looking at so intently. After a couple of minutes, the grandfather turns to the boy and points to the bottom of the cup.

"There is where Santo Pepe performed his miracles," his grandfather says. The boy cautiously peers into the cup, expecting to behold some vision so incredible that he prepares himself to drop to his knees. But all he sees is nothing, except for a few washed-out grounds of coffee.

The coffee grounds tell Santo Pepe's story. The little town of Las Flores was known for its wonderful sweet sugar cane. The town was completely surrounded by tall fields, and it was the sweetest sugar cane grown anywhere. Everyone in town was somehow connected with the sugar cane: as owners, planters, harvesters, or sugar makers. Everywhere you went, you would find people like happy termites, chewing on sticks of sugar cane, or like happy children, eating sweet bread, cookies, cakes, and candy, made from the sugar cane.

Then the town suddenly turned upside down. Some strange disease hit the sugar cane. In a few months, all the fields of cane rotted and died. Without the sugar cane, the people of Las Flores fell into darkness. Many left the town. Some committed suicide out of depression and desperation. Those who remained were inconsolable and barely kept alive, eating whatever they could find. They had been born and raised with sugar cane. With that now gone, it was as though their world had become a black grave.

One afternoon a man wearing a suit and tie came into town, carrying a briefcase in one hand and pulling a wagon behind him with the other. A strange metal contraption that looked like the engine of a rocket ship sat inside the wagon. He was a business man from up north, and he had come to town to open a café. He had heard about Las Flores from a friend of his, who had accidently stumbled upon the little town a couple of years back on his way south. His friend had described the town as full of the jolliest people, always high on sugar cane sugar. After difficult competition forced the man to close his café up north, he remembered his friend's story about

Las Flores and decided to open a café down there. Coffee, he thought, would go perfect with the sweet cakes and treats made from the sugar cane.

After walking about and exploring the town for an hour, the man realized that he had just traveled hundreds of miles for nothing. Instead of finding a town hopping with energetic and happy people, he found a tomb, and right in the middle of nowhere.

Tired from weeks of travel, the man needed to rest for at least two weeks and make a little money to get back north. To kill his boredom and have something to do while he rested, the man decided to set up a little outside café on one corner of the plaza and see what happened. He rented some chairs, tables, and other basic things. He also rented a bright yellow tent where he put his metal contraption and the jugs of water and coffee he needed to brew his coffee. After arranging his four little tables and chairs outside his little tent, he made a paper banner reading "Jaime's Café," with the words "Grand Opening" right below that. He hung the banner outside the tent, and then took a chair and sat underneath it, waiting for his very first customer.

He waited an hour, and nobody came. He waited a week, and still nobody came. Nobody even stopped by. It got to the point that Jaime broke down. He couldn't stand the silence, the lack of human contact. In desperation, he got the idea to walk door to door, begging people to come try his café. At least, if nothing else, he would finally get to see some people.

But as Jaime went from door to door, he found that nobody would open their door to him. They didn't even bother to ask who was knocking or what he wanted. He started to wonder whether all had died inside their houses, since he hardly saw anybody walking around outside anymore.

After knocking on thirty houses with no results, Jaime came upon a pink house with pink curtains. This house was unusual because it looked as though someone was keeping it up. The grass was cut, the porch swept, the flower beds and pots were watered. Every other house he had visited was run down, as though the people inside had just given up on living altogether.

After three knocks on the pink door of the pink house, Jaime turned to leave, expecting the usual non-response. But suddenly the door flew open, and Jaime found himself face to face with a big, tall woman with long hair, wearing a bright yellow dress with white shoes. Jaime was quite startled and forgot what he was supposed to be asking, or saying. He just stared at the woman and began moving his mouth up and down, without a making a sound.

The woman studied the strange man, who seemed as if he was just in from another planet, what with his suit and tie and polished shoes, as well as that constantly moving mouth, which said nothing. All of a sudden, as though hit by a bolt of lightning, the woman, who was named Josephina, jumped out and lifted Jaime off the ground in a big bear hug. She told him that, of course, she would marry him and why on earth had he taken so long to come? Jaime was stunned. He managed to pull himself out of the bear hug, but then fell backwards into a puddle of muddy water. Losing no time, Josephina reached out and yanked Jaime to his feet. She then planted a big kiss on his forehead, leaving a red imprint of her lips. Jaime made an awkward attempt to steady himself, and then said that there must be some terrible mistake since he was new in town and had never, ever met or seen Josephina before, in his entire life.

Jaime went on to explain how it was he came to Las Flores, about his café, and how desperate he was to get people to come to his café. Josephina then explained that, as for her, she had been praying for a husband for about a year now. She had been trying everything, from turning saints on their heads to losing weight. When she found Jaime at her door, she thought her prayers had finally been answered. After an awkward silence, the two broke down laughing. Josephina then said that she'd be delighted to be Jaime's first customer.

They walked down to the plaza together, and as they walked, Josephina told Jaime about the town, how wonderful things were before and how bad it was now. When they finally got to Jaime's Café, Josephina took a table and sat down. She commented on how she liked the yellow tent because it matched her yellow dress. She then asked for a menu. Jaime cleared his throat and said that there was no menu, that she could order either coffee or coffee with milk. In that case, Josephina replied, she would like a cup of black coffee.

Jaime quickly disappeared into the yellow tent, and after a while, he emerged with a tray carrying a big white cup and saucer. Josephina took the cup, and then took a sip. Jaime stepped back quickly, when he saw Josephina's round face puff up like a balloon. Josephina's face exploded, spitting coffee everywhere, onto the white tablecloth, the wall, on Jaime's tomato red face. Jaime stared in shock. Josephina then jumped up, smacked Jaime right between his eyes, and screamed that he was trying to poison her.

Jaime shook like a tamale leaf, and then took a sip of her coffee to show her that, of course, he was not trying to poison her. Eventually, Josephina calmed down. She then told him that his coffee was a disaster, that it was no wonder he had to close down his café up north, and that his café would never make it anywhere. Jaime looked so sad that Josephina finally took pity on him and asked him to show her how exactly he made his coffee.

Josephina followed Jaime into the yellow tent. He showed her the metal contraption that he had carried into town in the little wagon. He said that it was a coffee maker, and that he had picked it up on his way down to Las Flores. It was supposed to be the latest invention in coffee making, and after being driven to close his last café, he was determined to stay on top of the competition.

Josephina had never seen such a contraption. She looked it over carefully, as if it were a spaceship that had just landed from Mars. She then told Jaime to go ahead and show her how he made coffee using his strange machine. Jaime went through the steps one by one: carefully measuring water, coffee beans, putting them in certain containers in the coffee maker, and then finally switching the coffee maker on.

Josephina watched as the coffee maker hissed and shook. She then threw her arms up in the air when she saw the coffee maker producing a stream of pale brown dishwater liquid. She turned to Jaime and asked what was wrong with him, opening a café that only sold coffee and not knowing the first thing about making coffee. How did he ever expect to make a decent cup of coffee without first grinding the coffee beans before putting them into that stupid contraption of his? Jaime admitted that he thought his fancy coffee maker automatically ground the coffee beans, what with all he paid for it. Josephina left, but then returned with her hand coffee grinder from home.

She then helped Jaime make another pot of coffee. This pot was quite delicious. Jaime and Josephina sat at a table in the sunshine and drank cup after cup until they finished the entire pot. When Jaime finished his last cup, Josephina took his cup and peered into it. She then raised her eyes from the cup and told him that he should not leave town since his little café would do quite well. When Jaime asked how she knew this, Josephina simply pointed to the coffee grounds at the bottom of his cup. When Jaime still did not understand, Josephina spelled it out for him: She told him that she had read his fortune by examining the coffee grounds at the bottom of his cup.

Jaime was excited. He had an idea. He begged

Josephina to come work for him at the café. Josephina quickly said no, that she had no desire to spend her days making pot after pot of coffee, assuming that people did in fact start coming to the café. Jaime responded that she wouldn't have to brew even one tiny cup of coffee, that her job would simply be to read people's coffee grounds. Josephina quickly turned and read the coffee grounds sitting at the bottom of her cup, and then agreed to give it a try.

Just as Josephina foretold, business at the café picked up immediately. Word quickly spread that there was a strange metal contraption at the café that brewed magical coffee and gave people good fortunes. In a week, the entire town of Las Flores was drinking coffee at the café. Every day, lines several blocks long formed for a coveted cup of coffee at the café. Jaime could be found inside the yellow tent brewing pot after pot of coffee, while Josephina spent her time going from table to table looking into people's empty cups and telling them their fortunes. Within two weeks, the townspeople were back to smiling. People went back to work and play, and soon a new crop of sugar cane popped out of the ground. Before long, the town was back to chewing on sticks of sugar cane, just as before.

It was the coffee maker that put the town back in the saddle, and for this miracle, the townspeople bought the coffee maker from Jaime, named it Santo Pepe, since they didn't know of any other saint by that name, and started worshipping it. They eventually placed Santo Pepe in the town church alongside the other saints.

The boy sips the last of his coffee and then peers into his cup. He notices a few grounds of coffee at the bottom. He then hands his cup to his grandfather, asking him to please read his fortune. The old man takes the cup, looks into it, and then sets it back down on the table. He tells the boy to go outside and play in the sunshine, that his fortune is good, very good, that he'll always have happiness and love in his long life.

When the boy happily goes out to play, the old man cleans and dries Santo Pepe and then takes him back down to the basement, where he covers him up again with the white sheet. As he slowly walks back upstairs, feeling a bit winded and old, he wonders whether he'll still be around when the boy gets old enough to understand why he keeps Santo Pepe in the basement, why it is that he burns a candle each May 15 to Josephina. This is the day when Josephina finally married Jaime, the day he honors Josephina for the hope she brought to the town of Las Flores through her simple goodness and creativity, and especially for the magical life she created for him as his dear wife.

The *magdalenas*

They were going to Pepita's house. It was in Mexico, so they each had to pay a dime to walk across the bridge. It was always fun to see the Rio Grande River from on high. The water looked green with white foam.

Right in the middle of the bridge, the flags of the United States and Mexico stood and waved about three feet apart. The girl always wondered, when walking past them, which country owned the three feet of space.

She always knew when they got to the Mexican side of the bridge because suddenly a throng of young kids swarmed around them with small cellophane packages of gum, five square tablets to a package. The girl loved when her mother let her pick one. She always picked a package with red ones because they were hot and tasted like cinnamon. If the barefooted children were not selling packages of gum, they had marionettes, milk candy, or small piñatas to sell. The girl wondered if the children ever had time to play.

The girl and her mother came to Pepita's house every April, when the land was green and sprinkled with flowers. Pepita lived near the plaza, in a bright blue house with yellow windows. She had a little daughter named Gloria, who was three years old. Pepita had never been married. That was what the girl's mother told her when she once asked about Gloria's father.

When they opened the metal gate to Pepita's house, they found her outside. She was busy creating a relatively small right ear on a big, round five-foot paper head, using strips of newspaper dipped in a white flour paste. The large head sat on top of an old wooden picnic table. Piles of old newspapers and a large bowl of white paste mixture sat on a bench next to it. Jars of paints and a coffee can filled with paint brushes of all sizes were arranged neatly at one end of the table. A tall wooden pole draped with a white sheet leaned against the chicken-wire fence nearby.

Pepita was so happy to see them. She gave them a hug and poured them a glass of cold, red sweet water made from red hibiscus flowers. They sat on a bench by the picnic table and watched as Pepita finished working on the big head.

Once she finished with the ear, Pepita took one of the paint brushes, dipped it into a mixture of light brown paint, and started painting the little ear. She then carefully retouched the entire five-foot head.

It was the face of Pepita's grandmother: dark brown eyes, light brown hair, little ears. This was the only description she had of her grandmother, since she never met her, nor had her late mother, who died a year ago. Everything else about the face, including the thin, long nose and wide eyes, she made, using her own face as the model.

Later that evening, they would do what they did every year in April. They would accompany Pepita and her little girl, Gloria, to the church near the plaza. They would sit in one of the front pews and hear the priest talk about the *magdalenas*. They would then walk around the plaza three times. The girl and her mother would each carry a tall white candle in a paper skirt to catch the dripping hot wax. Pepita, with little Gloria beside her in a white dress, would carry her grandmother's five-foot head propped on top of a long wooden pole that was draped in a white sheet. There would be a total of twenty big heads on sticks. After three turns around the plaza, the procession of the big heads would continue to the cemetery, where the twenty *magdalenas* now finally rest, after being buried twice before.

The girl heard the story of the *magdalenas* when her mother brought her over to Pepita's house for the first time. Seeing the big head with the wide eyes and little ears caused the girl to break out crying. To her, the head looked like a monster doll, like one who would come at night to dance on her head. (Her mother had always cautioned the girl not to play with dolls at night since they were known to come alive and take to dancing on a girl's head once she fell asleep.) In an effort to calm the girl down, her mother explained that the big head was nothing to be afraid of, since it was only Pepita's grandmother, who was once known as Magdalena.

It turned out that Pepita's grandmother was only one of twenty *magdalenas*, each represented by a big head on a stick. All the *magdalenas* had once had their own real names, like everyone else. But their personal names were taken from them and then replaced with the name Magdalena when they first came to the convent nearby. They went there because they had no choice. They went there because they got with child and had no husband. They went there, had their babies, and then had their babies taken away from them. They were never told what happened to their daughters or sons.

And afterwards, the *magdalenas* were never able to leave the convent. They were forgotten. They spent the rest of their lives washing, ironing, and folding piles of never-ending laundry, from the wee hours of the morning to nightfall. They carried heavy buckets of water from the river. They cut down trees and chopped up wood to make fires to heat the washing water. Their work ended when they died. Each Magdalena was eventually buried in a small hill beside the convent, each in her separate wooden coffin. A small rock inscribed with the name Magdalena marked each of their graves.

Many years later, the convent sold the small hill to make some money. And right before the land changed hands, the convent dug up the graves of all the *magdalenas*. It then reburied them in a mass grave, with each Magdalena still in her own little coffin.

Nobody would have known about this had it not been for Raúl, a skinny old man who was quietly hired to help with the grave digging. Although he was a devout Catholic and was raised to have deep respect for the priest and the nuns of the convent, he found he could not sleep at night after digging up the *magdalenas* all day long. This went on for a couple of days until he finally broke down and decided not to participate in the digging anymore. He then mustered up the courage and went down to see José Rivera, a reporter for the local daily newspaper who covered births, deaths, weddings, and murders.

At first, José didn't believe a word of Raúl's story since he could not find anyone in town who knew anything about any *magdalenas* and because he was also raised Catholic and therefore could not believe that a convent was capable of such terrible things. But then Raúl started showing up at his office door early every morning. He would stand outside José's window and stare at him the entire day. This went on for days until José agreed to follow Raúl to the supposed grave sites, if only he promised to leave him alone.

When José realized what was going on, he started to investigate further. He then ran a front-page story in the newspaper the very next morning. The entire town was shocked. This generation of townspeople had never known about the *magdalenas*: how they had lost their names, their children, their families, and how they had lost their lives, working like slaves for the convent until they dropped dead, like invisible marked souls. They were appalled that the convent was now digging up the *magdalenas* and reburying them in a mass grave without making any effort to find and reunite them with their families.

At first, those at the convent refused to say anything

about the matter. But when they realized that the town was planning to cut off its financial and community support, they provided José with an old black book. The book contained some entries in faded ink, which turned out to be brief descriptions of each girl when she first came to the convent, before she was made a Magdalena.

One of the faded entries read: Isabel Gómez: sixteen years, dark brown eyes, light brown hair, little ears.

This was the clue Pepita used to help trace her grandmother.

❀ ❀ ❀

As the girl sat in the pew at the church later that evening, she noticed how so many of the women, who brought a big head on a stick, sat with small children next to them, with no father around, just like Pepita.

The priest blessed the twenty big heads on sticks that leaned against one side of the altar. He then read the real names of each of the *magdalenas* out loud. When the name Isabel Gómez was read, Pepita and her daughter Gloria bowed their heads and made the sign of the cross. The priest then turned and blessed the twenty women who brought the big heads on sticks, as well as their children.

As the parade of the big heads on sticks began, the girl smiled at the thought that little Gloria and the other children would never have to carry big heads on sticks to celebrate their mothers.

And later that evening, as she crossed the bridge back to the United States with her mother, the girl realized that the space between the two flags and the two countries didn't matter much so long as there was no space between her and her mother, who like Pepita's mother, never got to know hers.

The Woman with the Green Hair

The townspeople of Las Rosas called her "Irma" to her face, but referred to her as "the Bruja" (the witch) otherwise. She had bright green hair and eyes the color of clouds. She also wore the oddest combination of mismatched clothes, including shoes that never matched. Not only was Bruja quite peculiar in her looks, but she was forever running into walls, falling into holes, and crashing into people. The standard explanation she gave for her strange ways was that she was simply so highly evolved, so spiritual, that executing the ordinary physical aspects of everyday life was, well, beneath her. And, of course, this would be difficult, or rather impossible for others to comprehend since they were just ordinary people, or at least not as evolved as she was.

People eventually got so fed up with the Bruja's ways and her constant crashes into them that they banded together and started making fun of her. Every time they saw her coming down the street with a fresh black eye or a new sling for yet another mangled arm, they first tried immediately to get out of her way, and then they laughed at her, commenting that she would soon be giving the Almighty God competition, if her new physical wounds were any indication of her recent spiritual growth. At first, Bruja just turned her nose and looked away at such remarks, dismissing them as the patter of mere insects. But then she seemed to disappear altogether. Days went by without a single Bruja sighting.

Next thing you know, however, Bruja made the front

page of the local paper, announcing that José Castro, the town's mayor, was a big bug. When asked what she meant by this, she remarked that she had just received the extraordinary spiritual power to divine what people had been in their past lives by studying their hair. She had studied the mayor's hair when he was out at García Park yesterday giving one of his long and boring speeches, and found it to be aqua in color. That meant one thing and one thing only: that the little mayor had been a great big bug in his previous life. When asked what kind of bug, Bruja paused and then responded that she did not know exactly, but that she was quite sure it was not at the level of a butterfly, or even a moth or caterpillar. That a slug or cockroach was more like it.

This news immediately stirred up the little town. The mayor, who was running for reelection, took suddenly to wearing a hat everywhere he went. And when he got wind of Bruja's newest spiritual power, that of seeing through things like hats, the mayor, who had always been vain enough to boast about his pure Spanish blood, was reduced to shaving every last hair off his big round melon head. But it was too late. Ever since Bruja's pronouncement in the paper, the poor mayor lost every last straw of credibility. Wherever he showed up for a rally or a speech, the townspeople appeared in throngs and just laughed at him uproariously. They took to wearing T-shirts featuring a giant cockroach with the mayor's face. They also blew up huge balloons shaped like slugs and flew them on long, thin sticks over his bald head.

The mayor's opponent in the race, Juan Sánchez, started gaining a sizeable margin against the mayor by using the slogan "Experience as a cockroach or slug does not make for a good mayor! Vote for Sánchez, the man with real experience." Sánchez's lead was short-lived, however, when word got out that Bruja had just studied Sánchez's hair and she said he had no reason to make fun of the old mayor since he had been a toad himself. The debate around town became whether it was better to have been a cockroach or a toad, and the town was split down the middle.

Now when people encountered Bruja, they no longer dared to make fun of her. They, instead, made every attempt to hide from her. And when this was not possible, they tried, at least, to hide their hair and act nice by complimenting her strange outfits. Eventually, the townspeople became so paranoid about Bruja's new spiritual powers that one morning they just woke up and dyed their hair bright green, just like Bruja's. (It had been rumored that Bruja had recently been asked what she had been in her previous life, and after some thought, she nonchalantly responded that, of course, she had been Cleopatra. Wasn't that obvious, she added, what with her bright green hair?)

But when Bruja woke up to the bright green-haired town the next day, she immediately went to the local paper and issued a statement, saying that she couldn't be fooled. Just like she could see through hats, she could also see right through everyone's fake green hair. For example, she pointed to the reporter directly in front of her and noted that his real spiritual hair color was the color of a grapefruit, not the fake green he dyed it, and accordingly, he, without question, had not been Cleopatra, as he pretended, but a vampire bat, with extra long, hairy ears. And furthermore, she wanted the entire town to know that there was only one Cleopatra: her.

With this turn of events, the town shut down completely. Stores closed. Children stopped going to school. People got so scared of bumping into Bruja that hardly anyone left home anymore. The governor had to make an emergency trip to meet with the town leaders. After days of marathon meetings, the governor called all the townspeople together at the plaza and announced that a new law had just been enacted. The law required that by nine o'clock the next morning everyone, including children, had to have their heads shaved bald.

❀ ❀ ❀

When Bruja died three years later, from accidentally falling into a freshly dug grave that then became hers, the bald townspeople were shocked to discover that Irma's bright green hair was actually a wig and that she had been not only completely bald, all along, but completely blind as well.

The Tortilla

She opens her eyes and wonders whether she is really awake when she looks out her bedroom window and sees fifty people standing in a line. The line leads to the front door of Aunt Pepa's house next door. She wonders whether Pepa has died suddenly, bringing the people of their little South Texas barrio there to pay their last respects.

The young girl jumps out of bed and looks around for her grandmother. She finds her standing outside on the front porch, waving at some of the people in line.

The girl runs out and asks her grandmother how Pepa died. Her grandmother, startled by the question, laughs, saying that Pepa is more alive than ever. When the girl asks about the line of people, her grandmother laughs again and says that they are there to see the Virgin, the Virgin on the tortilla.

"What Virgin? On what tortilla?" the girl asks.

"Why don't you get in line and go see for yourself," the grandmother says.

The girl runs inside, splashes water on her face, jumps into her white summer dress, and then tries to tame her wild mess of curly hair with a large pink plastic comb. When she goes outside, she finds her grandmother sitting in her lime green metal chair, where she is eating a red apple.

"Well, tell me what you find out. Listen carefully to the people while you wait in line. They will give you clues," the grandmother says, as she reaches into her dress pocket and pulls out an apple for the girl.

The girl takes the apple to the end of the line. People are buzzing with excitement. All the girl can make out is that they are talking about some miracle and that the miracle has something to do with a tortilla.

The girl thinks that perhaps the miracle is that Pepa has finally learned how to cook. This would count as a miracle, of sorts, since Pepa's attempts at cooking had once almost killed her and three other people. Her reputation as a terrible cook plummeted to that of a toxic cook when she served soup at a dinner party made from mushrooms that had sprouted in her front yard after a rainstorm. The mushrooms turned out to be poisonous and they put her and her guests in the hospital for days. Afterwards, all she would say about the incident was that the soup was quite delicious. From then on, anytime there was a food fair for the church or a family get-together, Pepa was always assigned to bring the paper plates or napkins, never anything that could be eaten.

Well, the girl thinks, if somehow Pepa has learned to cook, it would be a miracle, and perhaps the Virgin on the tortilla is some special type of taco she's making in honor of the Virgin. Then the girl finally puts it all together: Pepa is opening a restaurant, which explains all the people.

But this explanation quickly falls apart when she hears a woman telling her friend that she is going to pray the rosary five times when she finally gets to see the Virgin on the tortilla. However miraculous Pepa's cooking now is, no one prays a rosary to a taco, the girl thinks.

As the girl observes the people more closely, she notices that a number of them are using crutches, wheelchairs, or look as though they're sick. The girl cannot make sense of what is going on. She turns to look at her grandmother, who is still sitting in her lime green metal chair, only now she is eating a banana. The grandmother catches sight of the girl and waves back at her. The girl shrugs her shoulders. She still hasn't a clue what's going on. Her grandmother just waves some more.

The line moves slowly. The girl notices three short round women leaving Pepa's house. As they walk past, people in line try talking to them. The three women all wear veils.

The girl continues to watch as the three women make their way down the line. They are coming closer and closer to where she is standing. They are making the sign of the cross and kissing the rosaries they carry. The girl catches her grandmother waving and smiling at the three women. Before they get close enough to where the girl can hear what they are saying, they walk away and head towards the girl's grandmother. The girl considers leaving the line and joining them, but when she turns to her grandmother, her grandmother shakes her head no. The girl watches as the three round women stand around her grandmother. They point to Pepa's house and raise their rosaries to the sky.

The line now moves too slowly for the girl. While her grandmother is absorbed in talking to the three women, she leaves her place in line and runs to Pepa's side door, which enters into the kitchen. The girl peers through the locked screen door, but is not able to see Pepa, or anybody else for that matter. No one seems to hear her when she calls out Pepa's name. The girl then climbs the tree nearby and enters the house through one of the kitchen windows. (She has learned this trick from Pepa herself, who has a tendency to lock herself out of her house and call on the girl to help her get in).

The girl climbs into the kitchen by first stepping on the kitchen sink. But then she catches her foot on a large bowl of white flour on the counter and crashes to the floor. A loud "alleluia" comes from the living room. Seven people suddenly run into the kitchen carrying rosaries. They stand there and stare at the girl, who is completely covered with white flour—hair, eyes, arms,

legs, her entire face. Pepa stares, too, looking quite bewil-
dered. But then she clasps her hands to her heart and
exclaims that the girl must be a little angel. The girl is so
stunned by her crash that she can't seem to speak. She
watches as the others look at her and at each other. One
whispers to the person next to her that she thinks the so-
called little angel is really just a little girl she has seen
playing in the neighborhood. But this is no time to con-
tradict Pepa, given the miracle and all.

Pepa takes the girl aside and leads her into the living
room. There, on a tall narrow wooden table, the girl sees
a big white vase filled with seven long-stemmed blood
red roses. Leaning against the vase is a giant tortilla, about
a-foot-and-a-half-round, and it has a great big burnt spot
right in the middle of it. Pepa drapes a white sheet over
the girl's shoulders and posts her right next to the tortilla.

Pepa stands on the other side of the tortilla with a
stopwatch in hand. She gives each person in line exactly
thirty seconds to view the tortilla. Once the allotted time
is over, she hits the person on the head with a long-
stemmed rose, signaling that it's time to move on. On
and on people come, one after another.

The girl watches as each person approaches the tortilla. They kneel, then they strain their eyes and look and
squint at the burnt spot on the tortilla. Pepa and the
seven or eight people still in the room then ask in unison,
"Do you see her? Do you see the Virgin?" Then follows
the invariable response, "Oh, yes, yes, I see her. Oh, my
God, there she is, the Virgin. It's a miracle." The girl
watches silently as the parade continues until nightfall.

Finally, Pepa turns to those at the doorway, saying
that she will open tomorrow morning at eight o'clock,
that they can see the Virgin on the tortilla then, and to
remember to say their prayers in the meantime.

"You were good, a real good angel. Let me make you
some hot chocolate," Pepa tells the girl, as she removes
the white sheet off the girl's shoulders. The girl's hair

and face are still covered with white flour. The girl finds enough in her to say that she'll take a glass of water instead. When Pepa returns with a glass of water, the girl only pretends to sip from it, as she asks Pepa where she got the tortilla.

Pepa says she had gotten up in the middle of the night craving hot flour tortillas with big chunks of butter, and since she could not ask any of her neighbors for a couple of tortillas, she decided to try making some herself. She took out the flour, the lard, and mixed the *masa*. She then turned on the griddle and rolled out the entire ball of *masa* into one great tortilla to save time. Well, the tortilla took up the whole griddle, and when she finally managed to flip it over, there it was — the image of the Holy Virgin Mary, right in the middle of the tortilla. She got so excited that she took the tortilla off the griddle without even cooking the other side of it and ran to show it to the girl's grandmother.

After examining the tortilla in the wee hours of the morning, the girl's grandmother had just shaken her head and gone back to sleep. Later that morning, Pepa went to mass, where the priest gave a sermon about how the Virgin had appeared to people throughout history and communicated with them in ways they could understand. At that point in the sermon, Pepa had suddenly stood up and announced to the entire congregation that the priest was really right about the Virgin communicating in ways people could understand, since the Virgin had just appeared to her that morning, right in the middle of the big tortilla she was trying to cook on the griddle. The priest tried to calm the congregation down, but five minutes later Pepa was leaving the church with twenty people in tow. After this, word of the miracle quickly spread, and soon people were lining up to see the Virgin.

The girl walks over to the tortilla and examines it closely. All she can make out is a great big burnt spot. She wonders whether that means she is bad, or at least not religious enough, since she cannot see any Virgin.

When the girl gets home, her grandmother is sitting on her old rocker, waiting for the girl's report. She laughs when she sees the girl all covered with flour, and then laughs harder when she hears that Pepa used her as an angel prop.

"Well, did you at least get to see the Virgin?" the grandmother asks.

"No. All I saw was a big burnt tortilla," the girl says. The girl then asks her grandmother whether she saw the Virgin when Pepa first brought the tortilla over. The grandmother just shrugs her shoulders. The girl then asks why all the other people are seeing the Virgin and not them.

"People see what they see, what they need to see, what they want to see," the grandmother responds. The next morning it gets only worse. The line outside is not only longer, but people are pitching tents on Pepa's front yard. A taco stand springs up over night. There are street vendors selling plastic rosaries, crucifixes, and other religious trinkets. There is even one selling a lamp contraption that plugs into the wall, in the shape of a white plastic tortilla with the image of the Virgin on it.

The girl joins her grandmother outside and sits on one of the porch steps. The grandmother tells the girl that Father Sánchez is due to come any minute to see what the commotion is all about. The grandmother also tells the girl that Pepa stopped by early in the morning to ask if she would come over and play the little angel again. But this time she preferred the girl to enter through the kitchen door, and so she left the key.

The girl tells her grandmother that Pepa is crazier than ever, and that she doesn't want to play the crazy angel part again. The girl's grandmother just smiles, and then says that it might be fun to see what the priest has to say about all of this.

The girl sits still for a while and then goes inside the house. She emerges ten minutes later, looking exactly as she did the day before, covered in flour from head to toe, and asks her grandmother for the key. She then enters Pepa's kitchen and peeks into the living room. There she finds Pepa, directing traffic again with her stopwatch. When Pepa sees the girl, she comes over and leads her to the bedroom, where she drapes the girl with the same white sheet. She then positions the "little angel" next to the tortilla, just as before.

About fifty people come and go for their allocated thirty seconds before Father Sánchez appears at the door. He shakes hands with Pepa and whispers something in her ear. Pepa then asks everyone in the room, except for the "little angel," to go outside so Father Sánchez can examine the tortilla in peace. Pepa then shuts the door and closes the shades in the room. Father Sánchez walks over to the girl and pets her on the head. He then peers into the tortilla. He opens his eyes. He closes them. He takes off his bifocals. He puts them back on. He picks up the great big tortilla and takes it to a lamp nearby. This goes on for half an hour. All the while, the line outside just gets longer and longer. Then the priest leaves, saying that he has to pray about this, that he will return tomorrow.

The girl hears the next day about the image of Saint Francis appearing on a tortilla across town. Then it's Christ himself, on another tortilla. But the biggest story is about one with the entire Last Supper on it, Jesus, the twelve apostles, a loaf of bread, and even a big goblet of wine.

The town gets so full of so many holy tortillas that no one goes to mass anymore. Everyone is at one of the holy tortilla sites. Father Sánchez eventually gets so fed up with the holy tortillas that he publishes a statement, saying that all the tortilla images are fake and so people are not to worship them anymore, and that to do so is nothing less than a mortal sin. That is how the line outside of

Pepa's house suddenly stops.

But three days don't pass before the line just as suddenly returns, and it is longer than ever. Apparently, while Pepa was not looking, a tiny old woman managed to break off a small piece of the tortilla and had then experienced a miraculous cure from some terrible cancer she thought she had.

The police is called to keep order at Pepa's house when fights break out over people's places in line, and two try to run off with the holy tortilla.

It gets to the point that Father Sánchez loses all control of his flock. He cannot convince the community to return to mass, regardless of how much he denounces Pepa and her "burnt tortilla." People start saying that there is more holiness in Pepa's so-called burnt tortilla than in all of Father Sánchez's store-bought, perfectly round, perfectly white hosts given out for communion.

Then one day Father Sánchez approaches Pepa and asks if she will start making tortillas to use as the communion hosts. From then on, people start attending mass again. Somehow, eating pieces of Pepa's burnt tortillas at communion every Sunday makes people better people — more hopeful, happier, as though they're connected to the Virgin, God, and so, no longer alone. When the girl finally brings herself to take communion one Sunday morning and almost gags trying to swallow the piece of Pepa's burnt tortilla that Father Sánchez places on her tongue, she smiles to think that her crazy Aunt Pepa is now known as the holy cook.

The *panadería*

There were fried, fluted fritters called *churros* and all kinds of wonderfully sweet smelling-cookies and *pan dulce* (puffy sweet breads) with humorous names and shapes: *conchas* (shells), *novias* (brides), *borregos* (sheep), covered with woolly coconut flakes, and *besos* (kisses), dough folded to form a pair of big lusty lips. There were special sweet breads baked to celebrate special holidays: *Buñuelos,* sticky fritters shaped like tortillas and sprinkled with cinnamon and sugar, were served with cups of frothy hot chocolate on Christmas Eve and in September to honor Mexico's independence from Spain. *Rosca de Reyes* (king's ring), a coffee-cake ring decorated with jewel-like candied fruits, was served on the eve of the Epiphany to welcome the three wise men. *Pan de muerto* (bread of the dead), topped with dough-shaped human bones, was offered to dead relatives during the Day of the Dead. And as for weddings, birthdays, saint days, and a girl's *quinceañera* (her coming-out party when turning fifteen) there were wonderful tiered chocolate, vanilla, and lemon cakes, large enough to feed almost the entire little rural village in northern Mexico.

The *panadería* (the bakery) was a tiny bright pink stucco building on a corner of the village square, with a large plate-glass window in front. Two long silver trays filled with the various sweet breads baked fresh that morning showed through the window like jewels and small sweet treasures. Inside, lining three sides of the *panadería,* were tall glass cases filled with shelves of the freshly baked cookies, sweet breads, and cakes.

The ritual always began at seven o'clock in the morning, when the doors of the *panadería* swung open. Then adult representatives from all families in the little village took turns coming inside and picking up a round tin tray and a pair of metal prongs. They would then feast their eyes and noses, like little children, on the magical sweet treats before them. With smiles on their faces, however early it was, they walked about the shelves, thoughtfully selecting an assortment of special treats, still warm from the oven, that their families would enjoy throughout the day. There were sweet baked breads to enjoy with *café con leche* in the morning and hot chocolate in the evening. Then there was the *merienda*, the afternoon ritual of enjoying a cup of coffee or hot chocolate and a piece of cake with friends to catch up on the day and with each other.

The creator of the magical sweet treats was Marta, who was thin and as tall as a broom, with obsidian eyes and a white cloud of hair. She was up each morning at four, measuring, mixing, and kneading. Her little kitchen was a flurry of sugar, raisins, cinnamon, chocolate, eggs, butter, vanilla, and flour. Once Marta placed the raw dough in her large oven, it was like magic. The dough transformed into breads, and the wonderful smell of baking bread wafted through the little village. The villagers loved waking up in the morning to the smell of the sweet baking bread and the anticipation of enjoying these treats throughout the day.

One Friday morning, however, the doors of the little *panadería* failed to swing open at seven o'clock. The trays in the window were empty, and the lights inside were out. Also, the village air smelled bitter and salty for the first time. The villagers who came, as always, to pick up the daily assortment of sweet breads for their families, were running around like ants on a hot sidewalk, not knowing what to do or think. They wondered whether

Marta was on vacation, but they had never known her to take a vacation, or any time off, for that matter. They then realized that they actually knew very little about Marta, other than that she baked the sweet breads they enjoyed. They then wondered how they could possibly go through the day, much less start it, without their sweet treats. They were so agitated that they called on the mayor to come see about the matter.

The mayor came, looked around, and then called on the sheriff. The sheriff came, looked around, and then called on Lola, the local psychic. But by that time, it was too late, because a little boy came flying out of a side window, saying that he had found Marta in her bed, that he thought she was dead, and asked how was he to get his sweet bread for his breakfast.

The autopsy revealed that Marta was killed by a cancer that was quite painful. The village was stunned. It couldn't seem to function without its sweet bread to cushion the nicks of everyday life and to celebrate the few good kicks life sometimes gave.

The village never got around to thinking about Marta, until a book was found while cleaning out her things. The book was thick and had a green cloth cover. It was filled with Marta's careful handwriting. She had written out, during the last days of her life, the recipe for every sweet bread, cookie, cake, and treat she had ever baked for the village. She had dedicated the book to them, to the souls of the people and to the well-being of the community, saying that she had gone on as long as she could, and that the village should not underestimate the importance of little things, such as the baking of sweet bread. She then added that after her husband and daughter were suddenly killed in an accident, she had moved to the little village and devoted herself to bringing joy and love to others through her simple baking of sweet bread, something she had done at home for the family she once had.

The village did not know what to think of Marta's book. But as the days after her death clicked on, the nicks of everyday living quickly chewed out the souls of the villagers, resulting in hot heads, fights, and overall unpleasantness. The worst victims were the children and the elderly, who took the brunt of the adults' unsatisfied sweet tooths and passion for sweet bread.

Then one early morning, the village abruptly woke up to the awful smell of something burning. The black smoke was traced to Marta's little *panadería*. There they found Juan and Julia, a couple in their eighties, and five young children. The kitchen was covered with spilled flour and cracked eggs. Charcoal black discs filled two cookie sheets.

Juan and Julia said that they were just trying to help. Their grandchildren had approached them and asked them to fill the air with the smell of sweet magic just like before, so that they and their parents could be happy again.

From then on, the village people organized themselves and took turns baking sweet breads and treats for the entire village each morning, with the use of Marta's recipes and kitchen.

To celebrate the memory of Marta during the Days of the Dead, the village baked and offered up to her an elaborate *pan de muerto,* and then named her the patron saint of their little village. It wasn't long before Marta also became known as the patron saint of bakers by the bakers in the surrounding villages. And when a baker named Julieta came to the village, asking if she could open a bakery there, the village welcomed her with open arms. They helped set her up in Marta's little *panadería,* and they treated her with the greatest warmth and respect, as though she had magical powers.

The Magician

Next to the bright pink pine coffin, which is decorated with lime green and orange paper flowers, is a long table draped with a black sheet. On it is a long-stemmed black rose, a wire cage with a little white sparrow painted to look like a dove, a deck of tattered cards, and a couple of bottles of tequila, each with a disgusting dead worm at the bottom.

The young boy tries to keep his eyes focused on his styrofoam cup with hot chocolate, but it is difficult not to steal a quick glance at the fantastic people sitting in a circle around the pink coffin. Next to his mother, who is sitting next to him, sits a big bald man, with a wild tangle of serpents, bursting flames, and monstrous gargoyle faces stenciled in blue ink all over his body, including his bald head. Directly across is an enormous woman, five-feet wide, wearing a bright orange satin costume, with what seem like long ostrich feathers sticking out all about her, which make her look like some unfinished parade float. The boy watches as she keeps jumping up and down, refilling her cup with more and more hot chocolate and stuffing her face with tamales, roast pig, beans, and the various assortment of cookies and cakes, which are laid out to look like the food table at some big wedding party. Sitting next to him is a man dressed like a clown, with pink cotton candy hair, except that his face is painted with large drops of blue tears and a big pink upside-down smile. A tiny man, with tiny chubby hands, and tiny purple shoes, sits next to the clown, with his feet dangling in the air. There are various other strange people sitting about, all wearing bright costumes and interesting-looking hats and plumes. The boy wonders why his mother insisted they dress all in black.

As he pounds the bottom of his empty cup to dislodge the four tiny white marshmallows that got stuck at the bottom, his mother nudges him to be still. Then he feels a tap on his right shoulder and sees the clown smiling at him with his upside-down smile, as he uses his long fingers to reach into his own cup to pull out a couple of tiny marshmallows, which he then ceremoniously pops into his big painted mouth. The boy stares at the clown, afraid to offend him, and then follows his example by also reaching into his cup and retrieving the little stubborn marshmallows. His mother told him that a funeral was a sad and solemn occasion; therefore, he was finding it hard to make sense of the clown, the loud carnival music that kept playing over and over again like some broken carousel music, and the fact that all the people about him seemed to think they were at a wedding, not a funeral.

The boy watches as people take turns kneeling before the open pink coffin, on a small wooden bench. The boy wonders what they all look at as they kneel there, since they all seem to smile as they peer into the coffin.

The boy wonders whether his mother will also go before the coffin and kneel there. He prays deeply that she will not insist he accompany her there. As the boy peers into his empty cup, the boy notices a full cup of hot chocolate being offered to him. He sees that the cup is offered by the sad clown, who is again smiling at him with his painted upside-down smile. The boy notices, as he accepts the cup, that the sad clown wears a ring with a pink stone on the middle finger of his right hand. This time around, the boy decides to swallow the tiny floating marshmallows as they naturally swim into his mouth. He doesn't want any more encounters with the sad clown, although he seems like a kind and attentive man, underneath his garish costume.

As he is about to finish his second cup of hot chocolate, his mother suddenly grabs hold of his hand and starts leading him towards the open coffin. The boy drags his feet, scared to come so close to death. He has never seen a real dead body before, and he pictures Uncle Felipe to be all bones, just like the skeleton candy he gets during the Day of the Dead. But when he kneels before the coffin and finally dares to open his eyes, at his mother's insistence, he is more shocked than ever. But it's not because Felipe is a pile of bones; it's rather that he looks healthier than anyone else in the room, including himself. Felipe is all in pink: beautiful pink suit, shiny pink buttons, a smart silk pink tie, and a pink rosebud in his lapel. He wears a ring with a pink stone on the middle finger of his right hand, which gently rests over his left hand, near his chest.

As his mother prays silently, eyes closed, the boy stares intently at death, at Felipe's rosy little cheeks and tiny rosy lips. The boy then suddenly jumps to his feet and tears out of the room. His mother, jolted, quickly makes the sign of the cross, takes to her feet, and rushes outside to find the boy. She finds him hyperventilating and deathly pale. She tries to calm the boy down, helping him regain control of his breath.

After about ten minutes, the boy's breathing is back to normal. The mother then extracts from the boy that he thinks Felipe is not dead at all, that he swears he just saw Felipe wink at him. The mother tells the boy to please settle down, to try showing more respect for the dead. She then reminds him that they are the only people there related to Felipe, that they mustn't make a bad impression. And since they are the only family members attending his funeral, they need to have a nice memory of it to tell their relatives back home in the city. She then takes him by the hand, and they return to the room with the pink coffin.

As the boy starts drinking his third cup of hot chocolate, he tells himself that perhaps the shock of seeing the
first dead person in his life caused his eyes to play a trick
on him. He, therefore, decides that he, in fact, never saw
Felipe wink at him. He then overhears the tiny man with
the chubby little hands laughing and telling a story
about Felipe and a pink wig of his that exploded into
flames, while attempting to light a match for one of his
magic tricks. It took three firemen and turning Felipe
into a giant sticky white marshmallow to finally put the
fire out. Then the enormous woman with the ostrich
feathers tells how one day Felipe almost closed down the
entire carnival when, instead of turning a huge tub of
sewage water into vintage wine, he accidentally turned
it into an enormous pile of shit. On and on the stories
come, like records in a jukebox, making the boy understand why Felipe and the little mangy carnival had to
keep on moving from one little obscure village to the
next. The boy then thinks that the telling of such stories
is quite an interesting way of showing respect for the
dead, even if it is true that his uncle was such a wacky
magician.

It then turns out that Felipe was actually killed by a
magic trick gone awry. While apparently attempting to
levitate a ratty old mule into thin air, the uncooperative
mule was only willing to go as far as elevating its two
hind legs to kick Felipe into more than thin air.

The boy then hears the sound of a bell and turns to
see a ten-foot-tall man ringing a tiny triangle with a tiny
metal stick, announcing that the procession to the cemetery is about to commence. As the boy rises from his
metal folding chair to follow his mother outside, he
quickly turns to give a last and final look at his Uncle
Felipe. He then abruptly trips and plows head first into
the back of the clown, after seeing Felipe's hands quickly switch positions, with his left hand now over his right

one. The sad clown again smiles with his upside-down smile, and gently helps the boy regain his balance. The boy, beside himself, whispers to his mother that he just saw Felipe's hands move. His mother shakes her head in reproach, insisting he settle down, and adding that sometimes dead people move, something like when wooden floors creak at night. It's just the body settling down.

Once outside, the boy watches as the pink coffin, now closed, is carried out by six of the strange people, with the sad clown in the lead. It is then carefully placed in back of an old wooden wagon that was painted pink to match the coffin. A mule with a goat standing on its back is hitched to the wagon. The boy wonders whether it's the same ratty old mule that kicked Felipe dead.

Then the procession begins. The boy and his mother walk directly behind the pink wagon as it is slowly being pulled by the mule. They walk silently, heads bowed, with their hands clasped in prayer before them; everyone else, however, follows in jumps, skips, and somersaults, playing horns, banging drums, and blowing bubbles and tin whistles. As they travel the half mile of dirt road to the village cemetery, the rest of the village eventually joins in, with children blowing comb whistles and adults banging spoons on metal pots and pans. The boy wonders why his uncle chose to be buried in this remote village where he knew no one and where he met his bizarre death. The boy is then suddenly overcome with a desire to have had a chance to know his Uncle Felipe, since even dead, he is the most amazing person he has ever encountered.

Upon reaching the cemetery, they find a family of seven, all in costumes of pink and green sparkles, running madly about, trying to chase three brown cows out of the cemetery. Once the cows are driven out into the road, the boy watches as the sparkling family takes to walking across a tightrope, which is suspended high over the hole dug for Felipe's coffin.

The boy listens to the prayers, which say something about rebirth, and then takes his turn tossing in a handful of moist dirt. They stay until two grave diggers, with three teeth combined, take shovels and pile in the rest of the dirt, until the hole is transformed into a little mound, which is then covered with all kinds of pink flowers, fresh, plastic, and paper. The last thing the boy remembers is the sad clown quietly coming up to him and presenting him with a little pink rosebud, saying how nice it was to finally meet him and how lucky Felipe was to have him for a nephew.

When the boy and his mother return the next day to the city by train, the boy watches as his mother quickly gathers all the immediate and extended family together and tells them about the beautiful funeral and burial of Felipe, who was her younger brother, and how everything was done first-class and formally. The boy is further perplexed when his mother turns directly to her father and informs him that Felipe was buried wearing a manly dark suit with big heavy boots, and that he had two bottles of real tequila, the ones with worms, buried in with him. They all then genuinely agree that it was really too bad Felipe was never home, that he was always traveling about, since he was the kindest and cleverest one in the family, even if he was a really terrible magician.

A week later, the boy's mother hands him a small box that came in the mail. In it, he finds a ring with a pink stone, like the one he saw on Felipe's right hand. Then a couple of days later, he hears a reporter on the radio announce that a carnival is coming to a village a distance away, featuring a new woman magician called Felipa, The Magnífica, who is the first known person ever to escape from sealed and chained boxes, even buried ones. The reporter then goes on to say that Felipa, the Magnífica, had just recently married a man she had known for a number of years and who worked as a clown. The boy's mother only smiles, when the boy shows her the pink ring and tells her about Felipa, The Magnífica—a smile he's able to understand only years later.

The Gold Clock

He cuts carefully. His silver school scissors follow the lines on the thick red construction paper.

He watches the others. There's Pedro. He's already finished cutting out one red boot. He's working on the other. Pedro brought a Christmas present for Miss Thomas this morning. It was wrapped in pretty silver paper, with a fresh red bow. He obviously had his mother wrap it for him, and he must be rich because the wrapping paper and the bow were new, not recycled.

Miss Thomas's eyes sparkled like Christmas lights when Pedro handed her the present. She put it under the little green Christmas tree on her desk. The tree has tiny glass ornament balls hanging on it, in all pretty colors. The tree stands next to her little gold clock.

He finally finishes cutting out the red boot. He starts on the second one. There's José. He's the talkative one. He told the boys at recess that Miss Thomas likes him, that he knows this because she never gets after him for talking and acting up. They told him that he's dreaming. But he's right, actually. All the boys hate him because Miss Thomas always laughs at his pranks. He mentioned getting her something really special for Christmas, like some nice perfume or something. Classy women, like Miss Thomas, like perfume. He wonders where one buys such perfume and how one knows what smell of perfume classy women, like Miss Thomas, like. He wonders whether his mother wore perfume, whether she was a classy woman, like Miss Thomas. He wonders what makes a woman classy. He wonders whether his mother wore perfume when they buried her.

Miss Thomas stops by his desk. She picks up the red boot he has cut out. She smiles, puts the boot back down, and walks on.

Heaven and peaches, that's what Miss Thomas smells like, he decides. Where do they sell perfume that smells like heaven and peaches?

Omar is laughing. He is the first to finish cutting out the two red boots. Miss Thomas tells him to wait for the others and then lets him go outside to get a drink of water.

He tries to hurry up and finish cutting out the second boot once he sees he's one of the last to finish. He looks over at the little Christmas tree. There are about ten gifts under it, all brightly wrapped. Tomorrow is the last day of school before Christmas break. He then starts sweating. Miss Thomas told the class not to bring her any Christmas presents, that all she wanted was for them to study hard and to behave, especially the boys. But he knew better. He knew that all his classmates were going to bring her a present and that they were going to get their mothers to wrap them for them.

Once everyone finishes cutting out two red boots, Miss Thomas shows them how to put Elmer's glue carefully around the edge of one boot except at the top, and then to paste the two boots together to make a Christmas stocking.

He likes the sweet sticky smell of the milky white glue. He likes how it dries and crusts on his fingers, forming a translucent second skin. And he likes peeling it off and seeing his fingerprints on it.

He wonders how he might go about asking his father for money to buy Miss Thomas a nice Christmas present. He knows his father will just laugh at him and say that he's either in love with Miss Thomas or he's a girl, since only girls do silly things like that. His father hates him, and with good reason. Didn't he kill his mother? She died giving birth to him. That's why he's always drinking, always in such a foul temper.

He wonders what Miss Thomas will think of him tomorrow when she realizes that everyone except him brought her a present. She will hate him and think he's selfish, just like his father does. Perhaps she'll just ignore him, pretend he doesn't exist, also like his father.

Miss Thomas passes a hole punch around. When it finally comes to him, he punches out four holes on the outer edge of the paper boot, as Miss Thomas showed them. The four holes make eight red construction paper circles that fall to the floor. He picks each of them up with his index finger.

He watches as Miss Thomas walks over to her desk at the front of the class and picks up her little gold clock. The clock is about three inches high, square, with a round face, Roman numerals, and it has a little yellow sun and a blue moon that rotate with the hours. She puts the little clock down and tells the class to hurry up since there are only ten minutes left before recess.

He watches as Miss Thomas takes out a ball of green yarn. She pulls out about a foot of yarn and cuts it off with the scissors. She then strings it through the holes of a paper boot, like a shoe lace, and ties a bow at the top. After this, she goes about the room cutting each of them a foot length of green yarn. He takes his and tries to follow Miss Thomas's example. He then finishes by writing his name on the boot stocking using Elmer's glue and sparkling silver glitter.

Then the bell rings. They all form a line at the back of the room. Miss Thomas leads them to the playground, where they are taken by Coach Taylor. The girls go with Coach White to play softball. The boys are told to run around the track. He hates to run. He starts slowly. Coach Taylor starts yelling to pick it up, that they look like a bunch of girls. He watches as the girls laugh and giggle out in the ballfield. One swings at the ball and misses, swings again and misses, then strikes out. She then starts laughing. He feels that he would've been humiliated. He wonders whether his mother played softball as a girl and whether she laughed when she struck out. He wonders whether she would've taught him to laugh if he ever struck out.

After recess, Miss Thomas goes to the playground and picks them up in a line. After a quick drink of water and a visit to the restrooms, they walk back to the room like a long centipede. Miss Thomas then plays Christmas carols on the record player. She gives each of them a piece of scotch tape and helps them hang their Christmas stockings by their cubbyholes. She then takes a big bag out of her desk and puts a large candy cane and a little Christmas book in each of their stockings.

The next morning Miss Thomas is agitated. She asks if anyone has seen her little brass clock. They all shake their heads.

After the Christmas party of green cupcakes with red sparkles, hot chocolate, and sugar cookies in shapes of stars, bells, and Christmas trees, the class makes Miss Thomas open her Christmas presents. There are scarves, bottles of perfume, flowers, fruit cakes, and boxes of chocolate candy. Towards the end, she stops unwrapping one of the presents and quickly starts on the next one until they're all opened. She thanks everyone for the beautiful presents, wishes them all a Merry Christmas and a Happy New Year, and then dismisses the class.

As the boy is about to leave the classroom, Miss Thomas calls him over to her desk. She then finishes unwrapping the present she had put aside earlier, and thanks him for the little gold clock, which she returns to its usual spot on her desk. She tells him that she knows it must be so hard for him not having a mother, especially around Christmas time. The boy looks down at the floor and starts to nod his head slowly, not knowing how to respond. Miss Thomas then takes the boy's right hand and puts the little gold clock in it. She tells the boy that she wants him to have it, to remind him that good things will also happen in his life, that time will somehow make things better. The boy then leaves with the little gold clock, which works to change his life forever.

The Wooden Chair

Cecilia's grandmother is whistling busy in the kitchen, preparing her most favorite meal of all—*cabrito en sangre,* which is kid, as in baby goat, cooked in its own blood. Cecilia thinks this a rather spooky meal, but she likes the great glee it brings to her grandmother, who was born and raised on a ranch, and so loves eating the most unusual things, like the eyeballs of cows, which she eats rolled up, one big greasy eyeball at a time, in a hot tortilla, and cow brains, as well as cow tongue, which comes rather long, with hundreds of bumpy taste buds. Cecilia has gotten to the point where she now doesn't even dare open the freezer door for a popsicle or ice cubes, especially after finding a whole row of shrunken heads, their big round eye sockets glaring out at her. When the girl screamed, running to tell her grandmother about the severed heads in the freezer, her grandmother had just thrown her head back in a roar of laughter, saying that those were tonight's dinner.

The kid-goat-in-blood dinner is one that the girl's grandmother only cooks on very special occasions, and this special occasion is the recent birth of the girl's little sister. Cecilia thinks it quite interesting that the arrival of her new kid sister is being honored with the cooking and eating of a baby goat in blood.

In the living room, relatives are soon gathering, congratulating Cecilia's mother and taking turns making sounds to the perplexed-looking baby. Some sound like birds, others like monkeys, and still others like water buffaloes, or what you would expect a water buffalo to sound like. There is laughter and noise and more noise. Cecilia is amazed to see how many people can fit in the small living room, but more amazed that a tiny baby, who can only wiggle and wiggle some more, just fascinates adults and reduces them to coos, goos, and moos.

Then her grandmother calls everyone to the table, as she carries a large white porcelain bowl filled to the top with the kid goat in blood. She places it carefully on the table, like some priceless offering to the gods. Everyone quickly takes a seat, and then deep white bowls filled with hot beans, rice, chile, and a stack of corn tortillas pass from one person to the next. The girl's grandmother walks around the table, ladling on each plate a big helping of kid goat in blood. They all immediately start devouring their food like starving alley cats, everyone, that is, except Cecilia, who just sits there, staring intently down at her plate, wondering exactly what part of the poor kid goat she has floating around in blood on her plate. She wonders whether the little goat was white or brown, and whether it even got big enough to grow a little goat beard. She next wonders how they managed to drain all its blood and put it inside the plastic bag she saw her grandmother carrying around earlier.

But Cecilia suddenly forgets about the kid goat when Tío Panchito bolts from his chair and tears out the front door, with her grandmother following close at his heels. Moments later, her grandmother returns and stares at the chair where Panchito was quietly sitting before.

"Where did this chair come from? Who brought this chair? Does anybody know?" she asks, as her eyes survey the circle of round faces sitting around the table. The chair is wood, carved, looks quite old, and smells like a stinky bat.

"Well, I did," Cecilia finally says, quietly.

"Where did you get this chair?"

"From the back alley. You said to go find some extra chairs, since we didn't have enough for everybody, so I got this one. I think somebody put it out for the trash people to take."

"Well, this little wooden chair almost killed your Tío Panchito. Did you know that? He claims it started rattling all of a sudden, right when he started talking to Elsa, telling her that, well, that he liked her new hairdo, that is, after she specifically asked him about it." Everyone's eyes then immediately turn to Elsa's hairdo, which, quite frankly, looks like a big bird nest, and not a very well-built one, at that.

The girl's grandmother then walks over and lowers herself down carefully into the old wooden chair. She turns over to Elsa, who is sitting immediately to her left, and says, "Where's the vulture? I mean, your hairdo, it looks like the bird nest of some scruffy vulture. You should immediately go and get your money back!"

Elsa instantly turns red and angry. But then Cecilia's grandmother just as quickly turns to her again and says, "No, really, I was just kidding. That's really a nice hairdo, and . . ." But before she is able to finish praising Elsa's hairdo, the wooden chair starts rattling and only stops when she stops talking.

Everyone has now completely forgotten about the kid goat in blood, as well as Cecilia's kid sister, and is totally captivated by the mysterious wooden chair.

"Do you want me to haul that old chair back out to the alley?" Cecilia asks, feeling bad that a whole lot of work went into cooking the kid in blood and birthing her kid sister and now no one seems the least bit interested in them.

"No, no!" they all say, as they then turn back to discussing the wooden chair. They wonder whether it's haunted, whether it starts rattling at the mention of a lie, since they all unanimously agree that Elsa's new hairdo is a colossal disaster. This instantly transforms Elsa into

a cyclone. She storms out the door, but not before proclaiming, in furious gusts, that she spent fifty dollars,
repeat, fifty dollars on her hair, which is more than any
of them make in a week, even combined, and that the
problem is not her hair, but the fact that they're all a
bunch of peasants—no, cannibals—who don't know the
first thing about taste, not even how to spell it, and
whose only concept of taste is killing and devouring, like
jungle animals, some poor little defenseless baby goat in
its own blood, and, moreover, that they wouldn't know
what taste was, even if it bit them, and bit them hard, on
their butts, big butts, which is the only real mystery
behind that stupid rattling chair.

The conversation then turns momentarily to whether
Elsa, with her new high-class airs that match her high-
class hairdo, is perhaps taking lessons on how to insult
others in a high-class manner, since that part about the
"butt" is new to them; they have never heard it used
quite that way before. And upon reflection, they all agree
that it is really quite an effective way of punctuating an
insult, and so they think they will now start incorporat-
ing it into their own insults.

Then they start wondering how to test the wooden
chair. Perhaps, it is only a coincidence that it rattles when
the person on it starts to lie. So they each take turns sitting on it, standing on it. Next, they get skinny people to
sit on it, then pleasantly plump ones. Old and young
ones. They even lay the newborn baby on it. But they
conclude that it only rattles when the person sitting on it
lies.

Before the night is over, they decide to invite Father
Kelly over to the celebration dinner. Father Kelly is a
young priest, recently transferred to the local church to
replace old Father Ávila, who is returning to Spain to
retire. All of them recall Father Kelly saying in his sermon, just last Sunday, that he wanted to go out and get
to know his community, in their homes, schools, and

places of work and play. He had also curiously mentioned that he wanted more and more of them to start coming to confession. How did they ever expect to be forgiven if they didn't even bother to stop by to confess their sins? And as for the complaint he has heard rattling about that it takes too long to even think about going to confession, what with the lines, the heat, the flies, and especially the severe penances meted out, not to mention that other piece of gossip about some poor old man who finally went to confession, after twenty years, and suffered a heart attack when he got sentenced, not only to one hundred "Our Fathers," but also to seventy-five "Hail Marys," well, all he had to say about all that was that it was his church now, it was a new beginning, a new day. As proof, he was guaranteeing that they would be in and out of confession as fast as they were in and out of one of those convenience stores he always saw them at, buying some cold drink in some huge plastic container, and, incidentally, he wanted them all to know that in hell, which, by the way, is much, much hotter, there are no little convenience stores where they can stop and get a cold drink to cool off, not even one in a tiny Dixie paper cup.

Well, Father Kelly is called, and true to his word, he actually stops by around eight o'clock. He smiles and coos at the baby, saying that he looks forward to baptizing her. He then greets and shakes hands with everybody, even takes a sip of red wine. But when it comes time to sampling the kid in blood, he turns as white as the pope.

But Cecilia's grandmother is undaunted. She politely asks Father Kelly to please sit down, all the while pulling out the old wooden chair for him. Father Kelly hesitantly complies, but not before looking around the room and noticing a number of far more comfortable chairs he'd clearly prefer. Once seated, Cecilia's grandmother again takes to insisting that he must take a little bite, however small, of the special celebration meal, since how else is he to get acquainted with the special delicacies of his new church community?

Well, Father Kelly, still white as the pope, starts stammering and then says that the dish looks, well, really quite interesting, rather, quite delicious, but, you know, his stomach . . . Then the chair starts up again, rattling and shaking. The priest jumps up and then jumps under the table, insisting that everyone take cover, that he was not told, when accepting this new parish, that there were earthquakes in this part of the country.

After dragging Father Kelly out from under the table and fixing him up in a big, comfy upholstered chair with a big glass of strong red wine, they recount the experiences they've had with the old wooden chair. Upon hearing all this and finally feeling satisfied that there's no earthquake and that his newly acquainted parish members are not completely mad, despite their bizarre celebration dinners, he gets up from his comfortable chair and walks over to the wooden chair. He picks it up, puts it down, walks around it several times, and then startles everyone present by announcing that he finally gets it now, that the wooden chair is actually a gift from God, that God has just answered his prayers.

At first, they all think the priest has had a little bit too much to drink, but then they really have no opportunity to formulate a second thought, because the next thing they see is Father Kelly throwing the chair over his shoulder and heading out the door with it. As he leaves, he turns his head, saying that if they are wondering about the chair, they will just, well, have to come to confession.

And there the very next day, they find Father Kelly hard at work in his confession box. Surprisingly, though, people are going in and coming out of confession in about thirty seconds flat. When Cecilia then accompanies her grandmother into the confession box, her grandmother discovers that she's sitting on the old wooden chair. She immediately starts laughing and is soon joined by Father Kelly, who is sitting on the other side of the confession screen. Father Kelly then quickly reminds her, as he says he has since warned all others, that she better confess truthfully, not forgetting little sins or embellishing others to seem like some big shot, since, as she well knows, the wooden chair she's sitting on will immediately start rattling at the mere whisper of a lie.

After Cecilia's grandmother darts off a quick "Hail Mary" for making fun of Elsa's hairdo, they walk home by way of the back alley, with the grandmother saying that perhaps they'll find another gift from God. And when they finally get home, Cecilia shows her grandmother the three loose floor boards where the old wooden chair had stood and rattled the night before.

Acknowledgments

I thank my family, especially my late father Antonio, my mother Dora, my sister Verónica, and my dear friend Pam, for their love and support.

Viola Canales, a native of McAllen, Texas, is a graduate of Harvard College and Harvard Law School. She was a captain in the U.S. Army and has worked as a litigation and trial attorney. In 1994, President Bill Clinton appointed her to the U.S. Small Business Administration, where she oversaw the delivery of economic and entrepreneurial development programs for various southwestern states. She currently lives in Stanford, California.

Ms. Canales also wrote *The Tequila Worm* (Random House, 2005).